BOOK TWO OF THE STORY OF US SERIES

THE REAL WORLD

THE ENTANGLED UNIVERSE

S.L. Harris

authorHOUSE®

AuthorHouse™
1663 Liberty Drive
Bloomington, IN 47403
www.authorhouse.com
Phone: 1 (800) 839-8640

Published by AuthorHouse 10/13/2018

ISBN: 978-1-5462-6406-4 (sc)
ISBN: 978-1-5462-6405-7 (e)

Library of Congress Control Number: 2018912245

Print information available on the last page.

CONTENTS

Dedication vii

Acknowledgment ix

Chapter 1:   Time to Act 1
Chapter 2:   The Set Up 7
Chapter 3:   The Call from the Hospital 11
Chapter 4:   The Grand Opening (It All Comes Together)....... 13
Chapter 5:   Closing Shop 20
Chapter 6:   Kelvin's Thoughts.. 24
Chapter 7:   William's Research 27
Chapter 8:   Sabine's Transition.. 30
Chapter 9:   Lamar's Help... 33
Chapter 10:   Samantha's Appointment with
              Dr. Virginia Desmond................................... 37
Chapter 11:   Insight into History.. 40
Chapter 12:   William's Lost Love 45
Chapter 13:   Malik's Visit to the Hospital............................. 48
Chapter 14:   William's Sexy Night.. 51
Chapter 15:   Breakfast at the Café 53
Chapter 16:   The Entangled Universe 58
Chapter 17:   Session with Amanda.. 62
Chapter 18:   Sunday Dinner 68
Chapter 19:   Lovers' Spat 73
Chapter 20:   Lunch Date 76
Chapter 21:   William's Work 82
Chapter 22:   Sexy Night.. 86
Chapter 23:   Mysterious Situation 89
Chapter 24:   Kelvin's Frustration 93
Chapter 25:   William's Remorse/Paranoia 100

Chapter 26:   The Work Day 103
Chapter 27:   The Session with Amanda 107
Chapter 28:   Kelvin's Unexpected Guest 113
Chapter 29:   Dinner with William..117
Chapter 30:   Meeting at the Cafe... 121
Chapter 31:   William's Reiki Session... 125
Chapter 32:   Kelvin's Return Home.. 130
Chapter 33:   Reflection.. 133
Chapter 34:   The Revelation 135

Note from the Author 139

DEDICATION

I dedicate this book to Grethel Ruth Brown, my fairy godmother, mentor, and coach. You are appreciated beyond measure. The impact you've made on my life is incredible.
I love you.
S. L. Harris

ACKNOWLEDGMENT

Thank you to my family, my friends, and for all of those who have taken the time to read my book and blogs. I love you and appreciate you so much!
S.L. Harris

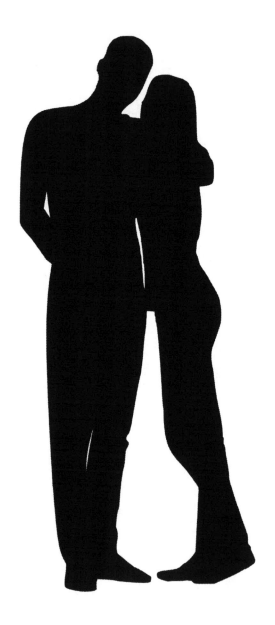

"You can hear me without words because
our souls speak to each other."
— Kelvin Frey

CHAPTER 1

TIME TO ACT

SAMANTHA

What a day yesterday, Samantha thinks.

On the one hand, it was a great day, the building met OSHA standards, Mrs. Gloria Wilson approved the inspection of the café, and they are due to open tonight at seven. Samantha thinks to herself, *One thing I know for sure is that Mrs. Wilson was accurate in her remark, "Now all of the real work begins." The preparation stage is over, it is time to act now…Heaven knows I don't work well under stress. Good thing that's my sister's specialty.*

Yesterday, Samantha and Sabine became the owners of S & S Café and Lounge, which was inspired by a dream their parents had of opening their own diner.

Well, Mom and Dad, wherever you are, out there in the universe, your legacy continues through Sabine and me.

Sabine has an uncanny ability to do her best work when there is a short deadline. So, Sammie is confident that the food will be divine and the decorations will be gorgeous. Sammie is all about preparing over time. She did more of the legwork over the months of getting the business up and running, such as setting up the interviews, going through a comprehensive checklist of the qualities she and Sabine felt would embody a stellar employee in a more intimate café setting, posting positions, buying supplies, working with vendors to negotiate the best deals, and working with contractors to get the space up to code. That was all easy for her. She's a natural at organizing and structuring things. However, this time, her organizational planning served two purposes: one, to prepare for the opening of the café and two, to keep her mind occupied from what was really bugging her, that she is losing her husband, Malik.

It's like everything she had blocked out in the last few months had come back full force: Malik. Casey. The affair.

I can do this, I can do this is what she keeps telling herself. *Face your fears, Samantha.*

She doesn't know if she has the energy to participate in the grand opening of the cafe. She barely has enough energy to get out of the bed, shower, and go to the café to meet the cable guy. She needs to be there between the time slot of nine and eleven to wait on the cable installer to get there. *I can never understand why they have such a huge window of time. Surely their technicians should be skilled enough and have enough confidence of when a job will be finished so that they can give actual times for appointments. A simple 9:45 a.m. would've sufficed for me. Aagh! I am so moody.*

As Samantha walk to the bathroom to get herself together, she glanced at the clock. It read 5:55 a.m. She knows Sabine has been up for at least three hours already, cooking and getting her mind right to decorate for the grand opening of the café.

In the recent past up until now, Sammie was able to hide behind the business and the preparation that came with it. Now there is no way to avoid this situation anymore. She thinks, *Damn, Casey's salon is literally right next door to our café. What are the odds of that? What are the odds of a woman whom my husband has known since his childhood randomly popping back up into his life years later and with an agenda?*

As she brushed her teeth, showered, and put on her clothes, it seems that she is in a perpetual haze. *Be in the moment, focus on your task,* she must keep reminding herself. There is a part of her that knows she needs to explore her feelings, but her mind keeps going back to flashes of conversations—well, more like arguments—she and Malik had, and she keep just skipping the exploring her feelings part and jumping right into making a decision part. *I need to make an appointment with Sabine. Hey, that's the benefit of having a sister as a counselor,* she thinks to herself. *If I could just hide in my feelings a little longer, that would be great. I know it's inevitable I'll have to face this situation sooner or later. I can feel that empty pull in my heart starting to come back. It feels as if my heart is dropping inside of me.* Her eyes started to water as she remembered the conversation and arguments she and Malik had over the past months.

"Pull it together, Samantha Marcs," she whispered to herself.

As she finished up in the bathroom, she stumbled across a little note from Malik in the middle of their two sinks with a box next to the note that was covered by a towel. The note read,

> *I know we are going through a rough patch, Sammie, but my love for you is always strong. We'll get through this, I promise. The box has a little token of my appreciation and love for you.*
>
> *Happy Birthday!*
>
> *Malik*

She stared at the note for several seconds, then she grabbed the box, walked out of the room and threw it in her purse without looking at its contents.

As she warmed up a bagel, she thought, *How did this woman get so intertwined into our lives in such a short time? I mean, really, can my situation get any worse? What are the odds of a woman whom my husband confessed to sleeping with days before our marriage having a salon right next to our café? What did I do in my life to deserve this? I am ruminating Sabine would say.*

Malik is out of town visiting with his mom—a much-needed break for them. He will be back in time for the grand opening tonight. He has been so distant lately. Whatever is in that little box, is his way of trying to bridge them together again. *It's going to take a whole lot more than material things to make this work,* Sammie thinks. *It feels as if I am living with a ghost now. I guess all of the disagreements get to a person after a while. Me accusing him of cheating, him denying the allegations…This seems to be the way of life for us now. Things use to be so different. It was so loving and peaceful between us. Now my days are filled with questions about how did it come to this.* What makes the situation even more bizarre is that she nor Malik can answer that question. One day they were talking about having babies and being together forever, the next day she woke up to a whole different man.

Then, when she tried to make amends and was open to keeping things fresh, thinking that's what their relationship needed. She introduced him to Club Enticement, a swinger's club. Things went even further downhill after that. Whatever Casey slipped into Malik's drink at that club scared Malik so much he couldn't keep the lie up, and he admitted his infidelity more than just before their wedding but a second and third time after they were married. He admitted that when Sammie and her sister were at the resort preparing for the wedding, something happened between him and Casey.

The day of his confession, when he returned from the hospital after having his stomach pumped, he was so scared. It was like a wakeup call for him. Samantha knew the situation got real for Malik. Actually, to say he is scared really is an understatement, he's more like petrified. *I guess I wasn't the most supportive person after he admitted his actions, but hey, what did he expect?* Sammie recalled the conversation they had yesterday after she came home from the walkthrough of the inspection of the café, after getting her hair done at Mz. Ingram's salon.

"Sammie, your hair looks good," Malik stated casually, turning the television down as he sat up to take a closer look.

"You think?" she asked sarcastically.

"Yeah," he answered hesitantly. "What's wrong? Why did you say it like that?"

"What's Casey's last name?" she asked.

"Oh, so we're back on that subject again?" He rolled his eyes.

"I don't care if I bring it up one hundred times, you owe it to me to talk about it. What's her full name?" she said loudly and slowly, enunciating each syllable.

Malik rolled his eyes for a second time. "Casey Sabryna Ingram," he stated. "Are you about to investigate her now?"

"It's too late. I should have done that months ago."

"What are you talking about Samantha?"

"So, you like my hair?" she asked calmly, swinging it from side to side.

Malik nodded. "Yeah. So?"

"Well, sweetheart…" she said slowly, "I got it done at Mz. Ingram's salon." she paused and looked at him.

"What?" he asked, perplexed.

"Casey has a salon right next to our café. And today, before I found out about the location, we signed a five-year lease."

Samantha called her sister as she left the house, she was thinking that she knows Sabine is probably concerned about her emotional health lately. She's been to herself a lot these past few months. Sabine is normally her sounding board, the one who can bring her back to center when she's traveled all the way off base. Sammie hasn't wanted to concern her lately with her marital issues, especially since it seems as if Sabine has met her where-have-you-been-all-my-life guy, Kelvin. They're developing a future together, and Sammie's wondering if her future with her husband of one year and three months is falling apart.

"Hi, girl. Happy birthday," Sabine exclaimed across the phone.

"Hey, girl. Happy b-day to you too," Sammie replied to her twin sister.

"So, how are you feeling?" Sabine asked.

"*Umm.* I don't know. A mixture of emotions. Happy, ecstatic, shocked. That's where I'm at right now. I haven't processed past yesterday after the news we heard at the hairdresser."

"I know, girl. It's a mess. Casey is a hot mess. Everything

happens for a reason. Plus, you know we can't have a divine time without the devil trying to crash the party," Sabine said.

"Just like in my dream." Samantha replied, matter-of-factly.

"Oh, yeah, right. The dream." Sabine relayed sadly.

Samantha could tell that Sabine's thoughts had taken her back to that horrid morning when Sammie vented her dream in scene-by-scene detail to her, Sabine chalked it up as jitters about opening the café, being newly married, and Casey being in the mix lately, but they both know now it was much more than that.

"Well, I am on my way over to the café to wait on the cable guy," Samantha said, breaking the silence looming between the two of them as their thoughts took them backward looking in hindsight at what transpired over the course of a few months in regards to Casey.

"Okay. I already dropped off some of the pastries that will be sold tonight. The caterers will be there throughout the day to set up, so it's good you'll be there. I'm finishing the last of the baked goods now. I have to go pick up a few more decorations. It's going to be a great day, Samantha. Focus on the moment every step of the way. We'll deal with everything that comes up as it comes up together."

"Okay, girl. I'll see you soon."

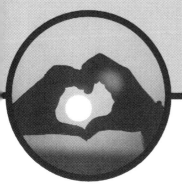

CHAPTER 2

THE SET UP

SABINE

I've got the cakes, pies, honey crisp biscuits, strawberry tarts, cookies, and croissants, Sabine thinks to herself. *It seems I'm good to go.*

Sabine packed everything neatly into the car, then ran back to the house to ensure that she didn't leave anything. She grabbed her purse and keys and locked the house. As she was driving over to the café for the second time that morning, she admitted to herself that she was a little disturbed by the fact that Casey's salon is right next door to their café. This is the same woman who allegedly slept with her sister's husband, put some type of voodoo on her new-found friend, William, and threatened her relationship with her fiancé, Kelvin.

In hindsight, Sammie's dream was more like insight into the situation with Casey. Sabine remembers it all too vividly, as if it was her dream instead of her sister's. Casey showed up to the grand opening invading Sabine and Sammie's space, then she morphed into Sammie. When Sabine reached out to touch her, she felt so much pain. At the time Sammie had the dream, Sabine chalked it up to Sammie being nervous about being newly married and them opening a business. Now, she see it was way more than that. Sabina thinks, *I need to go to that spiritual shop downtown to pick up some more crystals, incense, and amber oil and see if they have something with gusto to protect us from this woman's wrath.* Just as she thinks that thought her phone rings. It's William.

She answered, "Hi."

"Hi, love. How's it going?"

"William, did you know Casey owned a salon?" Sabina asked suspiciously.

"Yes. She talked about some of the workers from time to time; Michelle and Michael."

"Uh-huh."

"Why? What's up?" William questioned.

"You ever been there?" She asked.

"No," he responded.

"Listen, why don't you come over to the café? I'll text the address to you. I have something to show you."

"Okay. I'll be there. I was calling to see if you needed any help today. I know it's your big day—the grand opening. Plus, I want to repay the favor of you helping me out with the Halloween party."

"Well, thank you. I'm on my way there now. Meet me there?" Sabine asked.

"That's what friends are for, Sabine. However you want to use me is fine by me." Sabine can sense William is smiling, and she can't help the smile that comes across her face.

"You're so charming, William."

"Am I charming enough to talk you out of marrying Kelvin?" he asked.

"I'm hanging up now," she replied, shocked and tickled at the same time.

"Sabine. Sabine. I was kidding. You know I'm happy for you, right?"

"I guess," she said hesitantly with a smile.

"I am. I want you to be happy, and if Kelvin makes you happy...well, I have to live with it. I'll see you soon. Bye, love." William hung up the phone.

When Sabine get to the café, she spotted Sammie's car parked in front of the building. As she walk up to the window to look in, Sammie's nowhere in sight. Sabine unlocked the door and walked inside.

"Sammie?" she yelled.

Nothing.

Sabine pulled out her cell phone. Just as she was about to push the call button, Sammie walked out of the restroom and is at the top of the stairs drying her hands with a paper towel.

"Hey, girl," she called. "When did you get here?"

"I just got here. Can you help me get some of these desserts out of the car?"

"Yeah," she said as she walked down the stairs. As they were walking out of the door, William pulled up in his black BMW. He stepped out of the car wearing jeans and a polo shirt, walked up to them with a box in both hands, handing one to Sammie and one to Sabine. "Happy birthday, ladies!" He smiled.

"Awww," Sammie said. "So sweet."

"How did you know, William?" Sabine asked, curious.

"I have my sources." He smirked. "Open them," he said, rushing them.

Sammie and Sabine untied neat bright pink ribbons on top of each of the boxes. When they open them, there is a gold necklace for Sabine with the letter "S" as a charm hanging from it and a silver necklace for Sammie with the same charm of an "S."

"Wow," both Sammie and Sabine said in unison.

"Here, let me help you two put them on. I figure it's a good luck charm for you two. Plus it distinguishes you as the owners of this wonderful business S & S Café and Lounge. It could stand for Sabine and Sammie or for sexy and smart. You can use the names interchangeably."

Sammie and Sabine both smiled as he hooked one necklace and then the other around their necks. They both hugged him.

After pulling away from the hug, William looked up, "Aww, who knew, the font of the letters on the necklaces matches with your sign." William grinned and walked with Sabine toward her car. She handed off trays of desserts to Sammie and William, then they all walked inside. They set the trays down on the counter where the registers were located. Sabine put on some gloves to arrange the desserts in the display case, then she asked William, "So, did you see the name of the business next door?"

"No. I didn't pay attention. Should I go look?" he asked.

"Yes. Please," Sabine stated calmly, continuing to place desserts artistically on the upper and lower portions of the dessert case. Sammie busied herself with the cable guy who had just shown up to install the internet, cable and phone service. As Sabine placed the last dessert in the casing, she stepped back and admired the wonderfully decorated pastries. Sabine walked into the kitchen to take the gloves off and throw them away, then rinsed her hands. After placing the remaining cakes and pies in the refrigerator, William walked back into the building slowly, took a seat, then said, "You have got to be kidding me."

Sabine just shook her head.

"Sabine, you should have hired me to do some digging on your neighbors... Well, I guess you didn't know me back then," he said.

"Not much we can do now. We just signed a five-year lease for this place," she stated calmly, yet she could hear the irritation in her own voice as she spoke the words.

"There might be something. I need to find out how long Casey has had her cosmetology license. Those have to be renewed every two years, and they do background checks. The board can deny her now that she has a criminal record." William stood. "I've got some work to do. I'll be here tonight for the opening." He walked over toward Sabine and planted a slow kiss on her cheek a half an inch away from her lips. "No worries, Sabine. Let me do some digging, see what I can find out. Happy birthday, love." Sabine stood there and watched William exit the café just as the caterer and her team pulled up to the front.

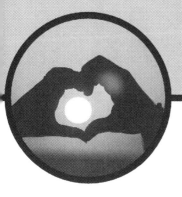

CHAPTER 3

THE CALL FROM THE HOSPITAL

"Hello. Mrs. Marcs?" the voice on the other end of the phone blared through the loud speaker of Samantha's car as they were driving back to the café for the grand opening.

"Yes. May I help you?" Samantha responded.

"I'm Dr. Virginia Desmond from the research department at Florida Hospital. I'm a part of the investigation of the club poisoning of Malik Marcs." Samantha paused and listened intently. "I've tried to reach your husband without success."

"He's out of town," Samantha responded. "Plus, he doesn't answer unknown calls."

"I've gotta tell you, this is the first time I've been at a loss as to what caused your husband's sickness that night. I've been doing this kind of work for ten years now, but I'm happy to report that we've gotten to the bottom of it," the doctor said proudly.

"Do I need to come in?" Sammie questioned.

Sabine could feel Sammie's anxiety as she was sitting inches away from her in the car.

"I would like to schedule a time where we could sit down and talk, but for now, I can read the results of the test over the phone if you're okay with that," Dr. Desmond said. Sammie and Sabine heard her rambling through papers.

"I'm okay with it," Samantha responded.

"The test showed that Mr. Marcs had methylene cyclopropyl acetic acid in his blood stream, which we term MCPA. This is very toxic Mrs. Marcs." She paused, waiting on Sammie to respond.

Finally Samantha asked, "How did this get into his system?"

"It was ingested. Most likely through the drink Mr. Marcs had at the club. MCPA is converted in the body. It's caused by a toxin called hypoglycin A, which comes about with the ingestion of unripe ackee fruit."

"Ackee fruit?" Samantha parroted.

"Yes, Ackee fruit is known in Jamaica as Jamaican vomiting sickness or ackee poisoning. The symptoms are similar to Reye's syndrome: vomiting, altered mental state, unconsciousness, coma, and death. It's a good thing you got Mr. Marcs to the hospital when you did." She said, feeling proud of herself that she'd cracked her part of the case. "Why don't you come in tomorrow around noon and I can provide paperwork, and explain more in detail to you?" she said, closing the conversation.

"Okay."

"Just come to the main entrance of the hospital and let them know you have an appointment with me. They'll page me to the front. See you then."

"Bye."

Sabine looked at Samantha after she hung up the phone. They had just pulled up to the café. Samantha was in a daze, then she said, "You know, I knew Casey poisoned Malik, but to get confirmation is beyond disturbing."

Sabine responded, "It is, but at least we know our suspicions are true and this goes into the police report. Malik is okay now, and that's what matters, right?"

"Yeah," she responded. "I need a minute."

Sabine got out of the car to give Sammie some needed space to process.

CHAPTER 4

THE GRAND OPENING (IT ALL COMES TOGETHER)

SABINE

It was two hours until the opening. As Sabine walked into the café, she was greeted by Julissa and Wendy, two of the new employees, who had been putting the finishing touches together for the party. They had the door prizes ready, and they were very excited. Sabine was excited also, but nervous at the same time. Everything appeared perfect. The caterer did a wonderful job preparing and setting up the hors d'oeuvres, and Lydia and Lamar, the other half of the staff, did a good job of helping them to arrange everything. There was an array of bacon-covered scallops; chicken bites; tortilla pinwheels; cheese sticks; grilled pineapple BBQ shrimp bites; cranberry pinot noir meatballs; sour cream, chive, and bacon deviled eggs; pepper-jack and bacon-stuffed cherry tomatoes; sweet potato bites; and parmesan pretzel bites.

The café was decorated out of this world. There are gold and silver streamers hanging from the ceiling, gold and silver balloons filled with helium floating around with curly strings and little weights on the bottom working against the helium enough so the balloons don't ascend too far from the ground.

Sabine's showcase of desserts looked beautiful. The deejay had set up his equipment off to the side of what Sabine called the dining room. It's the area where all of the long tables are located. The camera guy was setting up his section on the opposite side of the room. The cleaning crew did a wonderful job with making the place sparkle—Sabine thinks, *I might have to hire them permanently for nightly cleanups.*

Sabine could see their staff had everything together. It looked like this place had been here for years, and Julissa, Wendy, Lamar, and Lydia already felt like family. Sabine finally felt like she could breathe a sigh of relief. Yes, she worked very well under stress, but holding it all together takes a toll on her physically and emotionally. Sabine walked up the stairs and through the French doors to the office. She needed to relax a little before the opening. She walked past the desks Sammie had organized and set up so well. They had a fully functioning office with a fax machine, a copier, desk phones, and laptops. Sammie is so good. She pays attention to all of the small but important details. Sabine veered off to the left to the door of her counseling room. As she stepped inside, she closed it behind her and took a seat on the sofa. She took several deep breaths in and out. Tears instantly started to roll down her cheeks.

Sitting in the dark, she looked out of the window. She saw neighborhoods across the way, and the street lights added a dim glow to the counseling room. Minutes passed by like seconds. Her thoughts were taking her everywhere and nowhere at the same time.

She looked down at her phone and saw Kelvin had texted her. *I'm downstairs, baby. Where are you?*

She texted back, *Upstairs in my counseling room.* She hadn't seen Kelvin all day. He left late last night to go up to Jacksonville on business.

On my way up, he replied.

Minutes later, she heard the French doors open slowly, then heard him close the doors delicately behind him. She could hear Kelvin's shoes as they tapped against the hardwood floors. He paused for a second, then turned the doorknob. As soon as he opened it, Sabine stood, wiping the tears that wouldn't stop streaming from her eyes. Between her tears, she focused on the handsome sight before her. Kelvin was wearing a pencil-point gray suit that was tailored perfectly to his tall and slender body. He had on gray pants, a gray vest, and an asphalt-gray shirt with a tie that had sparkles of a metallic silver splashed in to an abstract design across it.

He looked at Sabine briefly trying to get a read on her, then he closed the door behind him without looking away. He walked over toward her, lifted her chin up to his face and stared into her eyes for seconds not saying a word. His face was vibrant yet etched with concern. His lips were thick and lusciously full, his goatee neatly shaven, and the hair on his head was thick and naturally curly. His light brown eyes seemed to be porting Sabine somewhere, the more she stared into them. She felt peace cover her entire body as if a soothing chill ran through her. Then her perspective shifted. She was no longer staring at his beautiful face. She saw herself standing there—puffy eyes, caramel-complected skin, smooth with light blush, and minimum lipstick, a glossy bronze outlining and filling in her heart-shaped lips. Her eyebrows were perfectly sculpted, and her hair was flowing around her neck and shoulders in loose curls, with the top portion pent up.

Then she heard a voice that wasn't Kelvin's, "These blessings I bestow upon you, Sabine. God has given his favor, and it is my honor to present this to you." The voice came back to her, and it was starting to resemble her late mom's voice. "As a human, you are afraid of the things that challenge you. It is your natural instinct to want to protect what is, the way it is right now. Growth requires expansion, and it is the hardest thing to do, sweetheart."

As she looked at herself and listened to this voice, which was so nurturing and so soothing, the tears continued to stream down her cheeks. It felt more like a release of fears.

"It isn't a matter of who you want to be in this world. It's a matter of who you've become. It isn't a matter of preparing anymore. It's a matter of being what you've prepared for. You've become a master of your own mind, body and soul. Be strong on your journey and know I'm proud of you."

In an instant, Sabine is back in this dimension—what she terms the third dimension, the rational reality. Her perspective had shifted back to staring into Kelvin's brown eyes.

There was a slight smile on his face before he asked, "Did you receive it?" Then his look turned very solemn.

She stared at him for a few more seconds, feeling better than she did before he came into the room.

"Yes," she responded, thinking, *If you're referring to the message that just came through to me in the sound of my late mother's voice.*

"So are you ready?" he asked calmly. She could tell his words were packed with so much more than the simplicity of them. He didn't just want to know if she was ready for this grand opening tonight. He wanted to know if she was ready to step into this new life that has been granted to her. The rites of passage as a co-owner of this café, as his wife to be, and any issue that arises as a result of this endeavor or the path that they are on together.

She paused, still looking at him, "Wait, what just happened?" she asked, still peddling backward, trying to process this other dimensional experience she'd just partaken in. She was simultaneously thinking of other experiences she had similar to this. They seemed to occur often since she and Kelvin met. In the few months she has known Kelvin, it had opened up some type of gateway that gave them easy access to the spirit world. Sabine feels that she is very much in tune with her intuition and consider herself to be advanced in her "clairs"—clairaudience, clairsentience, and clairvoyance. However, as of late, it was like a whole new source of communication had opened up to her through Kelvin and vice versa. It was a little unnerving at times, but she couldn't deny the peace and love she felt as a result of it.

"That's the result of our two hearts beating together in union," he said. "You can hear me without words because our souls speak to each other. I just wanted to deliver the message to you. Everything will be fine, Sabine. I don't want you to worry about tonight's opening, Casey's hair salon being next door, or wonder what I am going to think of the necklace you have on. I just want you to enjoy this time in this moment and each moment as it comes." He smiled as he touched the necklace William had given to her as a birthday gift, then he rubbed her bare shoulders and stood back to admire her outfit. Sabine was wearing an off-the-shoulder mauve dress with shimmers of bronze throughout it. It curved to her body but wasn't skin tight. The front portion stopped above her knees and the back came down a little below her heels.

"You look beautiful, baby," he stated softly and sincerely. He then wiped her tears away and kissed her lips gently. "Happy Birthday, Sabine. I'm happy to be by your side during this very special time. Come, I have a surprise for you." Kelvin took her hand pulling her out to the balcony to look down at the café. When she looked down, she saw the decorations that were set up earlier, the staff, the cameraman, the deejay, and Sammie who was walking up the stairs with Malik by her side. The only thing different was that on each table there was a bouquet of red and white roses and a banner across the top of the entrance that read, *Happy Birthday, Samantha and Sabine!* in gold letters.

Once Malik and Sammie reached the top of the stairs, the deejay put on a soft melody, and the six people below them started to sing "Happy Birthday." The cameraman came up to the stairwell and snapped pictures of all four of them. Julissa and Wendy scurried around and lifted a three-layer cake with white icing that read, *Happy Birthday and Congratulations, S & S* and walked it over to the bottom of the stairwell.

Sabine turned to kiss Kelvin on the lips. "Thank you, Kelvin. You're the best."

She then looked at Sammie and saw that she was smiling ear to ear. Sammie hugged Malik tightly, and Sabine could tell she was feeling grateful for him, especially after that phone call today from the hospital. Malik hugged Sabine and said happy birthday and Kelvin did the same to Sammie. They all walked down the stairs. Sammie and Sabine stood by the cake as the camera guy took more pictures. They blew out the candles and sliced pieces of cake for everyone.

The night was perfect. The turnout was great. It was casual and relaxed, and the food and music was wonderful. Looking around, Sabine noticed that all of the people on her email list showed up and that was well over 150 people. They sent invitations, however, the grand opening was open to the public, which included everyone they advertised to over the past few months. Some showed up with their coupon to get a free dessert.

"I guess all of our marketing ploys worked," Sabine whispered to Sammie as she helped to pack up and bag cakes and pies for their new customers.

"You think?" she asked sarcastically.

Out of the blue, a woman who looked vaguely familiar walked up. "Sabine, the turnout is great, and this place is really captivating. I tried some of the coconut pie, and darling, it is out of this world."

"Thank you. I'm so happy you enjoyed my little treats tonight," Sabine responded, looking at her trying to place where she'd seen her before.

The woman recognized that Sabine was a bit perplexed by her presence.

"You met me before...at Club Enticement. My name is Amanda." Sabine's mind took her back to that night at the club and the encounter in the restroom when Amanda spoke to her telepathically about Casey and her intentions not being good for her or her family.

"Yes, I remember you." Sabine walked closer to Amanda and gave her a hug. "You gave me some good advice that night. But, how did you know about the situation with Casey?"

Amanda smiled warmly, then reached into her purse and pulled out a card that read life coach and spiritual medium and handed it to Sabine. "I dreamt about you. My guides led me to you that night. You're coming into a new phase of your life right now, and you have some help from the other side."

"Wow," Sabine said, stunned as she looked at the card.

"Call me tomorrow. Maybe we can meet up and I can fill you in on some things." Amanda held up her bag of goodies that she had just purchased from the café. "I'll be munching on these all night. I'll talk to you later."

Sabine waved to her and watched as she exited the café.

Shortly after her exit, William walked up and put his arm around Sabina's waist. "So, are you feeling accomplished?" he asked.

Sabine smiled and wrapped her arm around his waist, as she looked out into the crowd and saw her staff working diligently to ring customers up and pack up goodies. "Very," she replied.

"I'm proud of you," William said, then he echoed Sabine's words to him from a few days ago on how he handled his father's death, the firm, and his emotions in general during that time. "You've handled this process gracefully."

Sabine smiled at him and squeezed his waist tightly as if saying thank you.

"I'm going to head out. It's late, and I have court in the morning and some research to do." She looked at the clock. It read 10:50 p.m. William kissed her on the hand then said, "Talk to you later, love."

CHAPTER 5

CLOSING SHOP

The party was dwindling down. People were exiting the café. Lydia, the manager, had turned the sign on the door to "closed" and had locked the front door. There were about twenty people left inside, standing in line to purchase baked goods. The desserts in the casing were also dwindling. It was a good thing Sabine had more pastries, cakes, and pies in the refrigerator in the back.

Sabine walked over to Julissa. "Can you help me refill the dessert casing for the morning?" she asked.

"Sure," she said as she walked with her toward the kitchen. Lydia and Wendy were at the two cash registers ringing people up. Before Julissa was interrupted by Sabine, she was helping with bagging. After washing their hands Sabine pulled out an assortment of pastries, cakes and pies, put some gloves on and began slicing and packing the individual slices into plastic containers.

Wendy walked into the kitchen several minutes later and said, "Wow. It was a great turnout! The last customer just left. The cleaning crew just got here." She grabbed some of the pastries that were just placed in the plastic containers and walked them out to the front then neatly arranged them in the casing.

It was amazing to Sabine how the crew knew exactly what to do. The café portion of the business was totally under control. Sabine informed both Julissa and Wendy on where all of the supplies and groceries were located, seeing as to how they would be doing the majority of the cooking. She gave them the grand official tour of the kitchen—from the gourmet coffees and teas to the cups and containers.

"We have to figure out the menu for the rest of the week. Today is Wednesday. We need a menu for Thursday through Saturday. Can you guys help me come up with the main dish? We'll have a special each day of the week."

They both shake their heads as they listen intently. As Sabine thought of Julissa's wonderful letters of recommendations from Florida Technical College naming her the best baking and pastry chef in her class, and Wendy's letters of recommendations from people who had purchased her baked goods for more than twenty years.

"I know you both are creative in the kitchen, so tomorrow if you two want to whip up one of your special dishes, that would be great. I want this to feel like your café also, so just be creative and show me what you've got." Sabine smiled and they both reached out to hug her. They both seem excited about this new venture, just as much as Sabine and Sammie were.

Sammie walked into the kitchen. "Can I be a part of the love too?" She joined the group hug then pulled away. "So, are we ready for our first official day of work tomorrow?"

"Yes!" Julissa, Wendy, and Sabine said in unison.

"Cool." Sammie said.

"I'm coming in at 5:30 a.m. to familiarize myself with the stove and equipment. I'm going to make veggie quiches and bacon and cheese quiches. Julissa and Wendy, is eight a.m. good for you?" Sabine asked then looked at them.

"Perfect." Julissa said.

"Works for me," Wendy said.

"I'll work with Lydia and Lamar on the daily operations and procedures in the morning." As Sabine said this, she thought on their credentials. Lamar was a sophomore at USF studying interdisciplinary social science with a concentration in religious studies. He had three years of experience waiting tables. Lydia had more than twenty years of experience managing employees. She was a department head for fifteen years and had managed a coffee shop for over five years.

"Can you let them know the hours of operation?" Sammie asked.

"The café portion is opened from seven a.m. to five p.m. Mondays through Fridays and nine a.m. to three p.m. on Saturdays. We're closed on Sundays."

Lydia and Lamar entered the kitchen.

"This was a great first day," Sammie said with enthusiasm. "You guys were excellent." Then she gave everyone high fives. "We couldn't have picked a better crew." She walked over to a table where she looked to have stashed something, then handed each employee an envelope she had just retrieved. "This is just a token of appreciation. We couldn't have done this without you guys. Just look at it like your first bonus check." They each were given a hundred-dollar bill along with their name tag in the envelope Sammie handed to them. "I'll add you all to the payroll program sometime this week. For now, just make sure you sign in on the clipboard in the mornings so I can keep track of your hours. The money you just received is extra. You'll still be paid a full eight hours for your services tonight."

Lamar said, "I think I'm going to enjoy working here. Thank you for the bonus."

Julissa, Wendy, and Lydia paid their compliments also. Everyone said their goodbyes and Malik and Kelvin walked them to their cars around 11:40 p.m.

Sammie walked over to Sabine. "I put my two weeks' notice in at the massage studio," she said, "so I'll be in and out of the café tomorrow. I have like three clients. All in the morning, so I'll be in around eleven, and I have to leave out for my appointment at the hospital soon after."

Sabine added, "Yeah? I need to go collect a few of my things from my old office and turn the key back in to the landlord." Sabine put in her notice to vacate at the beginning of the month. "I need to have all of my stuff out by tomorrow." She didn't renew her lease—she had been renting month to month. "Kelvin said that he is going to have a couple of his drivers move my things out by noon tomorrow. So I will need to step out of the café then."

After the cleaning crew left, they closed the shop by locking up and putting the alarm on the building. Kelvin and Malik were outside waiting by the cars. It was 1:30 in the morning. When Sabine walked over to her car, Kelvin opened her door. She kissed him on the cheek, then lips. "See you at home, sexy man," she whispered before driving off.

After Sabine had showered and settled into bed, Kelvin sat on the edge and took one of her feet and began massaging with delicate care. She breathed out a sigh of relief. "Thank you," she said to him.

Kelvin responded, "Sabine, you deserve a foot massage every night, and so much more. The café is great. You and Sammie did a wonderful job on it. I'm so proud of you. What time are you going in tomorrow?"

"I'm making a few quiches in the morning. I need to be there by five-thirty."

"You only have a few hours to sleep. I'll wake you in the morning, baby," he said as he continued to massage her feet.

CHAPTER 6

KELVIN'S THOUGHTS

After Sabine was asleep, Kelvin opened his laptop and began to type...

She is beautiful but more than just outwardly. Her beauty comes from a space I can't find the vocabulary to convey the words. It's more of how I feel when I'm around or in her general vicinity. I've never felt so connected, so complete, so happy as when I'm around Sabine. I wonder if she can feel the surges of energy, the sparks of divinity that seem to connect so easily and run like fire across all of the nerve endings in my body. It's like I'm a part of something bigger than myself when we're together. My purpose for being is to be with her, we together make one whole. This is the best description I can express. If I compare it to how I felt before, I was in a sea of nothingness, doing things to get to a certain point to reach a certain goal. I've made a great success out of my life, building my own logistics business with my father and brother, but none of that success seems as fulfilling as this one.

Marrying Sabine would be like a dream come true—a dream I wasn't fully aware of until the day we met. It's that otherworldly shit that I've always been privy to. I just didn't like *feeling* everything. Sometimes the world is so hard to block out. The energies that people give off is so toxic. Most times I want to escape those feelings; other people's feelings that I can pick up instantly by just being around them. Sabine's energy offers a haven for me, a sort of fortress of solitude that doesn't stop what I am picking up on, but transmutes it to love.

I spent my life, up to now, trying to run from my gift, only to meet Sabine who has shown me, without any knowledge of her own, that love is the answer. All of the beliefs I had before, all of the things my ego told me about women, all the selfish acts I've undergone, the games I played, the emotional turmoil of arguing back and forth, breaking up and making up, feeling angered about how someone treated me, all that is just gone.

It didn't just happen overnight. It was a spiritual process leading up to this point. I prayed for a woman like Sabine. I recognize the part I played in my past relationships not working out. There's a small amount of doubt that creeps up every now and then. I wonder if I'm ready for such a big step. Marriage. I know I'm not one hundred percent over the things that happened in my past relationship with Jaysha. . . Jaysha. That feels like a different lifetime now. . . Jaysha, the woman I thought was my "forever woman". I'm on the road a lot now that I'm building up these new accounts for my trucking business, and trying to network with more logistics companies. It has given me time to think about my past relationships and my future with Sabine.

Sabine has been so patient with me. All these trips I make is a passive-aggressive way of running away from the feeling that is elicited every single time that I'm around or *in* Sabine. She is perfect. Well, nobody's perfect, but she's perfect for me. I guess one way of describing it is that meeting Sabine was a shock to my soul, and I need time to process it to know for sure.

All the knowledge my mother instilled in me about God and love came back to me. Like a book of knowledge, all the wisdom returned and began pouring down into my crown chakra, melting down to my third eye, filling my entire aura and then spilling out toward Sabine's aura. It is as refreshing as a cold glass of ice water after being in the desert for days without any liquids, or like that feeling of being in a hot shower and feeling the water beat against your skin after a cold winter day in Michigan. Like sitting in front of a warm fireplace on a cold snowy day. Nope, even with the description I just gave, it barely gives justice to what I'm trying to convey. There are no words. Just a feeling. A knowing. Love at its purest form.

All I know is that everything my mother said to me on *the day* she left this world, now makes sense on an emotional, mental, and spiritual level. She said things that my mind was not mature enough to comprehend at the time. I remember the words as if she spoke them yesterday. Me standing at her side as she seemed to pass from one dimension to another—she was in and out. Her sentences were broken and I thought, *This is it. She's talking crazy, and I'm losing my mom.* Little did I know it was just a transition from one phase of existence to another. Her words are still with me even as I think of that time, it plays in my head like a movie.

"You'll meet her one day, son. I've told you this before; you need to trust in love, go deeper than your ego, deeper than your fears, look past the illusion and see the truth. It will be a catalysis going on between you two. An activation of each other... an inner species connection that will directly link to a higher source, The God Source. The button will be pushed on all the dreams deferred. It will be about love and connection instead of fear and separation. Messages will be conveyed in all sorts of ways—visual, auditory, tactile, chemical, sound, pheromones. You two will be better together than apart. Remember, son, the purpose of each of our relationships is to evolve spiritually. We take everything with us is what I am finding out now. Our souls will remember the lessons from earth, which mostly has to do with emotions and limitation. It's for the expansion of our souls. But to meet your twin soul as a romantic partner is rare in a lifetime. You have evolved over seven lifetimes together as mates. It will be the love from the story of another life based on ancient soul memories." Then she smiled and took her last breath as I watched the life withdraw from her body. I felt chills and a breeze as if it was a release of her soul.

Kelvin reaches over and pull the covers up on Sabine, and kiss her on her forehead, then whisper, "I love you baby," before turning out the lamp on his side of the bed and putting his laptop away.

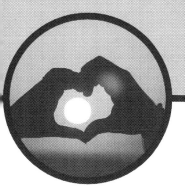

CHAPTER 7

WILLIAM'S RESEARCH

"Shit! This woman is crazier than I thought," William said out loud to himself as he logged off of the computer at two a.m. and walked over to his mini bar to pour himself a shot of bourbon.

Casey Sabryna Ingram born in Jamaica. Raised by her step-mother Nadine after the passing of her father, Samby Kaymar Ingram, witch doctor and Obeah prince. Williams thoughts are scattered as he think on the information that he's researched on Casey, trying to wrap the whole idea of her up in a summary. It's shocking to him that he's known her on a personal level for a while, but really didn't *know* her at all.

What the fuck is Obeah? William questioned, thinking of the Instagram video he watched earlier of Casey talking about bringing the Obeah religion back. William's mind kept taking him back to her Instagram message. Casey was sitting in a small room and spoke of the spiritual practices her father performed, some in the healing aspect and some in the black magic aspect.

"Alexa, what is Obeah?" William asks his virtual assistant, an Amazon product which rest as a speaker on his desk.

Alexa responded, "Obeah is a kind of sorcery practiced in the Caribbean. It is not a religion in the classical sense—no meeting place such as a church. Focused application of 'occult power.' Sanctioned to facilitate or induce spells. The practitioner is beyond the guidelines of traditional witchcraft, sorcery, shamanism, or voodoo."

After swallowing down the shot of bourbon, William looked over his notes. Casey was born in Jamaica. Samby, her father, died of an unknown illness. Her mother couldn't afford to keep her, so she gave her to Samby's mistress, Nadine. When Casey was six years old and relocated to the states, she lived with Nadine Johnson's family. From there, it looked like she went from house to house and eventually ended up in foster home after foster home.

Her attack on William was her first offense, legally, a battery, which was a felony with no priors or convictions. She would probably just get probation. If she was charged with poisoning Malik, that would be a felony charge to the first degree.

William used the restroom then went downstairs to his room to get a few hours of sleep before court in the morning. He has taken on a lot over the past few months with his father passing away and leaving the law firm to him, but with the help of his staff he has been able to stay afloat during this time. He has court in the morning on a case that he is closing out.

William made it to his office before noon after being in court for three hours. As he walked in, his assistant Tosha informed him he had a visitor who had been waiting patiently for him for more than an hour.

"She didn't have an appointment, and she wouldn't tell me her name. I tried to get her to schedule a meeting with you, but she refused," Tosha whispered.

"That's fine," William said, feeling groggy and tired after his late night and early morning. "Where is she?"

She pointed to the waiting area.

William strolled around the corner to find Casey waiting on him. She was sitting in one of the chairs with her legs crossed wearing black sunglasses. He walked over to her. "What are you doing here?"

"I came to see if you would be willing to drop the battery

charge," she stated boldly and with mild aggression as the words escaped her lips.

"Listen, Casey, that isn't going to happen. Plus, it looks as if you have bigger issues than a battery charge. I suggest you get some legal representation for court next month."

Just as William was finishing the last of his sentence, she stood and was a few inches away from his face when she said some words that weren't familiar to him. She walked past him, bumping his shoulder and exiting the office.

William stood there for a few minutes just processing the whole incident. The feeling that he had was not sitting well with him. He walked around to Tosha's desk.

"The woman who just came in is Casey Ingram. She has a battery charge as a result of my doing. She is not allowed on the premises. I will hold a meeting in thirty minutes about upping the security here. Please send a memo out via email for everyone to meet me in the conference room."

CHAPTER 8

SABINE'S TRANSITION

It was almost noon on a Thursday, and Sabine was rushing out of the café to meet Kelvin and his crew across town to get her files and personal things out of the old counseling office. Sabine was so exhausted. *It's not easy opening your own business,* she thinks to herself, *Well, if I could get to Sunday, then I'd have time to rest and reflect.* Saturday, she has a full schedule of clients to see—six appointments to be exact—starting first thing in the morning.

This morning things went exceptionally well. The crew and Sabine whipped up some great breakfast and lunch meals— breakfast bowls, quiches, sandwiches, spaghetti, homemade garlic bread, and salad. There had been constant customers in and out of the café. With the profits of the café, Sabine's counseling business, and Sammie's massage practice, she already knew business would be booming. They had three different practices in one building. Financially they were winning, yet now they had employees to pay and utilities that they were responsible for, but just looking at the sales from last night from the café alone, they brought in $4,500, which about covered everything that was spent out to make the grand opening a success.

Sammie and Sabine dished out about $88,800 for this business in total. That included the $10,800 they'd paid upfront to Bill, the landlord, as a down payment and $24,000 to get the renovations done, including furniture to make this site custom to their taste.

Now they had the remaining $54,000 to pay over a five-year time frame.

As Sabine pulled up to her old office space, she felt, as William termed it, accomplished. It made her proud that she had her own space. As she reflected on the past, she felt appreciative of where she'd come from, but ecstatic to be moving up in society as a business owner and not just a consumer anymore. She and Sammie had a business to call their own.

Sabine looked out of her car window and saw Kelvin standing by a U-Haul truck he'd rented. He was smiling at her. Two of the truck drivers who works for Frey Transportation, Kelvin's trucking company, were sitting at the curb. Kelvin walked over to Sabine's car.

"Hi, sweetie. You ready?" Kelvin asked.

She handed him the key to the building as she got out of the car.

"You know I've never been to your old counseling office before."

"I know. Do you still have the card I gave you with the address?" she asked, feeling nostalgic, thinking of the lunch date they'd had a few months back before she and Kelvin were engaged, celebrating their move in together.

Kelvin leaned against the car, reached for his wallet from his back pocket, then pulled the card out to show her.

Sabine smiled and walked over close to him. Their heads tilted, their lips touched. Sabine's skin tingled as if electric currents flowed through her nervous system, focusing at the point of contact he was making with her lips. All of a sudden, her legs felt weak. Kelvin sensed it as he grabbed her by the waist, pulling her in closer to him, deepening his kiss as this innocent gesture turned into something more erotic than it was intended to be.

Kelvin whispered seductively in her ear, "I can send the guys away for a few minutes and we can...you know, in your old office."

Sabine's eyes were closed because she knew if she opened them and gazed into his beautiful brown ones, whatever he requested, she'd grant. She engaged in a sweet yet passionate kiss once more with him, then pulled away to bring herself back to reality. This was her attempt to remain focused on the task at hand. When she opened her eyes, the two guys he'd brought with him to help move a few of her things were smiling and whistling at them.

Kelvin turned toward them and then back toward Sabine and grinned. He touched her hand then said, "To be continued, baby." He held the key up she'd given him minutes ago. "If you have everything labeled, I can handle it from here. I'll send you a video through the Marco Polo app to make sure we've got everything you need before we leave. Go back to the café, sweetie."

"You sure, Kelvin?" Sabine asked, sort of relieved he had committed to helping her move the last bit of the heavier items like the file cabinet, sofas, and end tables. "I don't want to feel like I'm just leaving you to do all of the work here."

"Sweetie, you're going to have to get use to me being around and helping you. That's part of my role, to take some of the stress off of you. I'm positive you can go. I'm sure you have a lot to do at the café."

"You are too good to me, Kelvin. I love you. Thank you," she said.

Kelvin kissed her once more and walked over to the guys explaining the plan. As she got back into her car, she got an incoming text message from William.

Call me, Sabine. It's important.

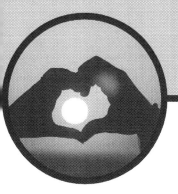

LAMAR'S HELP

SABINE

William met Sabine at the café. After their conversation over the phone during the car ride, she was curious about what William had found out about Casey. He was naturally calm and very levelheaded, and she usually had a very soothing and comforting experience when they interacted, but what he was saying over the phone had her a little freaked out.

"Hi, love," William said as he walked over to greet Sabine at one of the café tables. She pushed receipts aside and stood to hug him. He kissed her on the cheek.

"Hi. Are you okay?" Sabine asked, feeling his uneasiness as he took a seat right next to her, pulling his chair closer. He was dressed in a navy blue suit with a burgundy tie and smelled of Burberry cologne.

William began pulling out paperwork from his briefcase. Sabine saw highlights across words like *Obeah: Resurgence, Jamaican voodoo, West Indies religious practices,* and the likes.

"Casey came by the office today, wanting me to drop the battery charge," he said as he sorted through his paperwork.

"Could you do that if you wanted to?" she asked, looking back and forth at him and the paperwork he was meticulously organizing on the table.

"No. It is not up to me at this point. If I changed the story, I could be charged with filing a false police report. I don't think she really felt I would consider what she was asking of me. I think she was trying to threaten me."

"How?" she asked.

"Sabine, I'm feeling all kinds of things right now." William stopped organizing his papers and looked directly into her eyes. "You know how I felt that night I came over to your house, when I tried to explain to you the creepy shit I saw Casey do in my closet on the floor? —chanting in a different language, that icky feeling?" William continued searching for words to describe his first supernatural experience with Casey, his ex-lover, and Sabine's sister's husband, childhood friend.

Sabine placed both her hands over his to calm his soul down. She energetically communicated, without words, sending calming love vibes to him, remembering how he reacted during their counseling sessions when she would do deep meditations with him.

She whispered, "Safe place, William. Go there now."

He looked at her awkwardly. "What?" he asked.

"Go there now, please."

He closed his eyes and took a deep breath.

"Do you see the beach and the waves hitting the shoreline?" she asked in a soft tone.

"Yes, I do."

"Take a deep breath and release your fears. I don't want you freaking out right now. Remember that love is the most powerful force in the universe. Yes, Casey is acting out. She's working from a lower standpoint that operates and feeds on fear, but that isn't where we are right now. We're moving up, up, up. You're an observer. Don't get drawn in to the fear. I'm going to count backward from five, and you're going to come off the beach feeling protected, grounded, and safe. Five, four, three, two, one."

William opened his eyes, and he seemed more like himself now. "Thank you, Sabine. I needed that." He stared into Sabine's eyes for seconds as if he was getting his thoughts together on how to present what he was trying to communicate. "I did some research last night on Casey. She's practicing some type of Jamaican voodoo religion. She posted something on Instagram about Obeah." William paused. "Sabine, this is totally out of my league. I don't know what I'm dealing with here. It scares me on so many levels. I've hired security guards for my office because of Casey." William shook his head, sat back in the chair and let out a long breath.

A few seconds went by and Lamar, the guy Sammie and Sabine hired to wait tables, walked over. "I'm sorry to be eavesdropping," he said. "but I overheard you talking about voodoo."

William and Sabine looked at Lamar.

"Well, I know a little about this. My major is religious studies at the university."

"What are you, like twenty?" William asked, assessing Lamar, feeling that he's too young to know anything about this situation—it's hard for William to comprehend.

"I'll be twenty-one in a few weeks." Lamar nonchalantly grabbed a chair. "Do you mind?" he asked before he sits down.

Both William and Sabine shrugged.

"What do you know about this?" William asked professionally, like he was cross examining a witness.

"More than I probably should. I wrote a paper on the practices of voodoo across many cultures, specifically ritual magic in the Jamaican culture. It was brought over from Africa but is practiced in the Caribbean. Half of the people who are a part of this religion don't worship the dark forces, but they know they exist, and they realize people do use these dark forces," Lamar said.

William stared at Lamar for a little while, as if considering a proposition for him, then he asked, "Lamar, what is your schedule like?"

He answered, "I work here Monday through Friday from eight a.m. to five p.m. I have classes three nights a week—Monday, Wednesday, and Thursday and one class Saturday mornings."

William reached into his briefcase and pulled out a business card. "Call me tomorrow after work. If Sabine isn't against moonlighting, I may have a part-time gig for you, if you're interested."

William and Lamar looked over at Sabine.

"I'm okay with it," Sabine responded, then looked over at Lamar. "Just don't overload yourself. Your first priority should be school, okay?"

Lamar smiled. "Thank you," he said to Sabine and nodded.

CHAPTER 10

SAMANTHA'S APPOINTMENT WITH DR. VIRGINIA DESMOND

Samantha walked up to the information desk at the main entrance of the hospital at 12:05 p.m.

"Hi. My name is Samantha Marcs. I have an appointment with Dr. Desmond."

The lady behind the desk said, "Okay. Let me call down to her office."

Samantha feels that she and Malik are back to being sweet and supportive towards each other, yet they still can't talk about the elephant in the room every time they are together alone. They lay in bed and don't even touch each other. The concerning part about it is that Malik seems more afraid than defensive now, and Sammie feels the exact same way. In the recent past, Sammie has been so upset with her husband, thinking about how he brought Casey into their lives and all of the damage it has caused in such a small amount of time. All that keeps going through Sammie's mind is how she could have lost Malik that night at the club, and it brings her to tears every time.

Samantha haven't told him about the news from Dr. Desmond she received yesterday. She figured she'd wait until she spoke with the doctor in person first. Besides, she doesn't want his past relationship with Casey to interfere with evidence in the case. *As soon as I'm done here, I'm going down to the police station to provide this information to Detective Mack so we can get this case rolling,* Sammie thinks to herself.

Minutes later, a woman who looked like she is in her mid-thirties walked up to greet Samantha breaking her from her thoughts. She reached out to her. "Hello, Mrs. Marcs. I'm Virginia Desmond. Thank you for clearing your schedule to come see me today."

Samantha shook her extended hand. "No problem."

"Follow me to my office so we can talk."

She led Sammie down the hallway to an elevator that took them to a lower floor. After exiting the elevator, they walked past her lab, which was encased by glass, and into a small room that had papers everywhere stacked neatly on the floor and over the desk. She pulled a file from her drawer and opened it.

"Have a seat, Mrs. Marcs," she said as she flipped through the file. She pulled a summary sheet out and handed it to Samantha.

"This has been sent over to the police station already. All the other content is for you and Mr. Marcs to review." She handed the file over to Sammie. "Are you or your husband of Jamaican descent?" she asked.

"No," Sammie responded. "I was born and raised in Pensacola, Florida, and Malik was born and raised in Miami, Florida."

"Do you eat at Jamaican, Haitian, or African restaurants or have you traveled out of the country lately?" Dr. Desmond asked.

"No."

"You've heard of ackee rice and salt fish, right? It's a common Jamaican dish."

As she said this, Samantha's mind reverted to that day Casey showed up at their house unannounced and had cooked what she thought was salmon and yellow rice. Samantha's anger started to resurface as she thought about how that witch had the code to their home, which Malik had given to her a while back during the time she and Sabine were out of town preparing for the wedding. Samantha thinks, *There Casey was a few months ago, cooking ackee rice and salt fish without mine or Malik's knowledge in my damn apron, in my damn kitchen, in my damn house!* She threw all the food away that evening. Samantha was snapped out of her inner rage by Dr. Desmond's voice.

"Mrs. Marcs, are you okay?" she asked.

"What?" Samantha questioned, feeling sick to the stomach thinking about the danger that this woman impose. *It wasn't salmon and yellow rice.*

"You look faint. Do you need water?" The doctor got up and grabbed a room-temperature bottled water from her cabinet and handed it to her.

Samantha gulped down some swallows, yet she still felt lightheaded. "Do you have a rest room I can use?" she asked.

Dr. Desmond stood. "Yes, follow me." She led Sammie to the rest room, but before she could open the door, everything went black.

CHAPTER 11

INSIGHT INTO HISTORY

SABINE

Sabine pulled up to an expansive all-white house with a wraparound porch. As she exited her car, she saw several wind chimes dangling in the slight gusts of wind. She heard the light chimes that resonated in harmony with each other, playing a melody that only nature could create. It was so peaceful and enchanting. Walking up the stairs to Amanda's home seemed almost surreal, as if she was in a dream. *I feel like I've been here before*, she thinks. A sort of déjà vu hit her harder than she'd ever experienced. Amanda seems familiar to her also. When Sabine first met Amanda at *Club Enticement* it felt as if she had known her before. Amanda showed up to the grand opening of the café and now, here they are again.

"Sabine," Amanda called out from the other end of the porch.

Sabine walked over. Once she was near, she reached out to hug her. Amanda stood about five feet five inches tall, had light caramel skin; long, curly brown hair; and was wearing a lengthy, flowing pink-and-baby-blue dress. She had several silver necklaces dangling from her neck down over the curvature of her breasts all ending with a different color stone attached.

"This area is beautiful," Sabine said, after pulling away from the hug. She took a deeper look at her surroundings. They were outside on the porch. In front of them was a small outdoor table with two chairs. Straight ahead was a huge tree with beautiful green leaves. This tree looked exactly like Hawthorne, the tree Sabine had seen in her mind's eye as she meditated.

"It is beautiful. I love living here. Have a seat, sweetie." Amanda motioned to the small white table with two chairs.

The table had a pitcher of lemonade, two glasses, and a small plate of cookies. Sabine sat, and Amanda continued to speak.

"Help yourself to something to drink and cookies. Now, I have to warn you these cookies are not even halfway as delicious as the treats at S & S Café and Lounge. I'm a little embarrassed to report I ate all of my goodies."

She laughed so wholeheartedly that it made Sabine giggle.

Amanda touched Sabine's hand. "Sweetheart, I'm so glad you made it."

When she said this, the meaning behind her words echoed deeper with Sabine.

"The directions you provided were very straightforward. I'm accustomed to people giving me addresses and plugging that into the navigation system, but the landmarks you referenced were extremely helpful," Sabine said.

"Yes, yes." Amanda nodded. "If I gave you the address, it would take you off course. It's something with electronics and this space out here."

Sabine took a bite of the cookie and looked up. "Not bad." She then pulled out a small box from her purse and handed it to Amanda. "Tea cakes. They'll go perfect with this lemonade."

"Honey!" Amanda exclaimed. "Thank you. My mother—Naddie, is what I called her—used to make these." She bit into one. "They taste exactly the way I remember as a child." Her voice cracked a little. She seemed emotional thinking on a memory. "I'm sorry. Let's get started." Amanda pushed the box of tea cakes aside and said, "You've been here before, both you and your sister, Samantha. Almost thirty years ago." She handed Sabine a picture of her, Sammie, and their parents standing by the tree out in the yard.

Sabine rubbed her hand over her mom and dad's faces.

Then she handed Sabine another picture that had a woman and what looked like her two kids, and a much older man. When Sabine turned the picture over, *Rashida, age 13* and *Sabryna, age 6* was written on it. She looked up at Amanda.

"That's me, my mom, my stepsister, and stepfather," she said pointing out who was who on the picture. "My middle name is Rashida, I was 13 years old there."

Sabine nodded, handing the picture back to her.

The third picture she handed off had Sabine, Samantha, Amanda, and the youngest girl Sabryna on it.

"Wow! We knew each other," Sabine replied. She turned the picture over, and it showed *Sabine and Samantha, age 9; Sabryna, age 6;* and *Rashida, age 13.*

"Yes. Our parents knew each other," she responded. "We met a few times back in the day."

Amanda picked up her glass of lemonade and brought it to her lips, her eyes glazed over, and then, everything was still. Sabine noticed that she no longer heard the wind chimes or birds chirping. She didn't even feel a breeze. She took a deep breath and turned her head in Amanda's direction. When she looked into Amanda's glazed over eyes, she swirled into what felt like a vortex. All of a sudden, Sabine was outside of a barn at night. She saw a bonfire and people gathered around farther up, music playing in the background.

"Where am I?" she asked.

"In my memories, Sabine," a voice very faintly spoke.

"Am I supposed to be here?"

"You're allowed to know the truth, sweetheart," the voice whispered back to Sabine.

She walked around the barn and saw a baby goat with its neck slashed. It was still alive but kicking its legs around slowly losing life. As she walked inside of the barn, someone was crying. Sabine walked up a flight of stairs that led to a room of some sort. There was a young girl balled up in pain. The girl had a on a white gown, and there was blood all over the bottom of her gown and her legs. Sabine walk around her trying to understand this illusion and why she was having it.

Then she heard very weakly, "It's me, Amanda."

When Sabine looked to the young girl, her features did resemble Amanda's. All of a sudden three women entered the barn and they were rushing up the stairs to tend to the girl. The women had towels, water, and healing herbs. One woman had her hands over Amanda's belly and seemed to be energetically assessing the situation.

"What is it, Naomi Ruth?" another woman's voice called out.

The woman assessing Amanda was Sabine's mom. Sabine walked around and took a closer look at Naomi Ruth. She had beads of sweat on her forehead and was very focused on what she was doing.

"The baby is gone," Naomi Ruth finally said. "Hand me the herbs so we can stop the bleeding."

One lady was assisting by using towels to clean up some of the blood, and the other woman was rubbing Amanda's hair off her face and whispering calmly to her. Sabine's mom was grinding leaves and roots together.

Sabine came out of the memory Amanda allowed her to see. "You lost your baby?"

"Yes," Amanda said as she set the lemonade glass down. "I also lost my ability to bear children on that day."

"I'm so sorry," Sabine said.

"If your mom had not been there, I would have lost my life also." She paused then continued. "Your mom was a healer—the medicine woman. After my mother passed away, my stepdad wasn't much of a parent. I became pregnant four years from the time in the picture, and I miscarried in my eighth month."

"So you were seventeen?"

"Yes."

"Who was the father, if you don't mind me asking?"

"The man who was at the club with me the night we met, Steven. We remained friends all of these years."

"What did the goat represent?" Sabine asked.

"A goat symbolizes fertility."

"So, the neck of the goat being cut means…"

"My loss of fertility," Amanda said.

Sabine nodded. "I'm sorry for bringing it up again. Just trying to understand," Sabine trailed off.

"The more your ability grows, the more symbols you will see. You can decipher them later as you figure out their meanings."

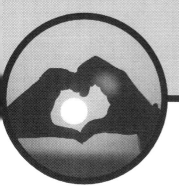

CHAPTER 12

WILLIAM'S LOST LOVE

SARA'S SIDE OF THE STORY

William pulled up to the tiki bar and exited the car confidently, strode inside and had a seat at the bar as he waited to meet up with Sara, his ex-girlfriend. He ordered a mai tai, anticipating the taste of orange-flavored rum on his tongue.

Moments later, Sara took a seat beside him. "I'll have what he's having," she said.

William turned to look at her. Even though he invited her here tonight, he couldn't believe she shown up. She was just as beautiful as the moment he laid eyes on her, in his last few months in law school. "Sara, you came."

"Of course. You invited me." She stared at him for a moment then asked, "So, I don't get a hug?"

He stood, reached over and wrapped his arms around her body tightly. She returned the gesture wholeheartedly. They sat and both sipped their mai tais.

"So...how's Casey?" she asked.

"Yeah, about that... She turned out to be the crazy, psycho bitch you said she was," William said matter-of-factly.

"Imagine that..." Sara said with a half-smile.

"I've missed you," William said.

Sara shrugged. "I would hope so. I would like to believe what we had was real. I still find it hard to believe you chose her over me."

William breathed in deeply and sipped more of his drink. "It wasn't like that, Sara."

"I know you, William. I know you love women, and she had just the right amount of charm, charisma and mystery about her, and that intrigued you. I just thought you would have a little fun, maybe a one-nighter, and that would be that, but, you moved the woman in with you. That was a shock and a slap in my face," Sara said, stirring her drink with a straw and staring at William without breaking her gaze before finally lowering her eyes to her drink.

"There's so much I want to tell you, Sara," William said, "but right now, I'm just so happy to see you. It's like we never skipped a beat. I'm so sorry for what I did to you. There's no excuse for my behavior." He looked at her with searching eyes.

"No worries, baby. You can make it up to me later," she said as she gripped William's thigh. "Plus, I heard through the grapevine that Crazy Casey is in some deep shit. Care to elaborate?"

"Yeah, well—it's a long story," William stated, remembering Sara's distaste of Casey from their experience in law school, and probably even more now that Sara perceived that Casey stole William from her. "Why did you hate Casey so much when we were in school?"

"As if you need to ask now. I mean you lived with the woman for a few months, you should know. I'm assuming the battery charge that was filed against her is from you?"

"Ah, yes," William said, remembering to whom he was talking to. Sara had definitely done her research.

"So, you understand why I call her Crazy Casey now?"

William nodded and tried to suppress a smile as he listened to his ex-girlfriend and fellow attorney lay the truth on him.

Sara began to explain how she and Casey were the best of friends in grad school for the first year, but as time went on, Casey started to drink a lot and her attitude seemed to change.

"I remember when we went on a three-day weekend retreat

to Jamaica—Montego Bay. It was nice—until Casey met up with these guys native to the area; one from the Cayman Islands and the other one from Haiti. She was acting so different." Sara stopped herself and drank the rest of her drink.

William changed the subject because even though part of his mission tonight is to find out more about Casey from Sara, the other part of his plans are starting to sink into his mind.

"So, are you dating anyone?"

She smiled then answered, "Wouldn't you like to know?" and raised her eyebrows.

"Actually, I wouldn't." William responded feeling his jealousy spike.

"Well, Mr. Witford, stop asking questions you really don't want an answer to."

"Noted," William said.

"I'm available tonight, if that's what you were getting at."

"My place?" William asked.

"Sure. I'll meet you there. I have to use the ladies' room."

"I could wait on you and walk you to your car…"

"I'd prefer if you went ahead and set the mood at your place," Sara said seductively.

"Got it. See you at my place in a few." William stood and helped Sara to her feet. She walked off purposely switching her hips as she knew William was watching her.

William waited for Sara to use the rest room and walked her to her car against her wishes.

"Always the gentleman," Sara said as she stared at William lovingly in the eyes, "I told you to go ahead of me and prepare."

"No worries," William replied as he watched her get into the car and closed her door.

CHAPTER 13

MALIK'S VISIT TO THE HOSPITAL

SAMANTHA AND MALIK

Samantha called Malik. "Baby, can you come pick me up from the hospital?"

"Uh? Hospital—what?"

"Malik, my phone is breaking up, but, yes. I'm at the hospital. Can you please come pick me up?"

"Okay. What's the—" Before Malik could finish his sentence, Sammie hung up on him. He looked at the phone then placed it in his pocket, walked into his manager's office and said, "I have an emergency. My wife is at the hospital."

His friend Leon jumped into the conversation before Malik's manager could reply. "Oh, is Samantha okay?"

"I don't know. She just called me and told me to come pick her up."

"Alright. How many do you have left to see?" Leon asked, referring to the number of patients scheduled for occupational therapy for the remainder of the day.

"Two," Malik responded.

"I got you. Go check on that beautiful wife of yours," Leon said as he took the files out of Malik's hands.

"Thanks, man." Malik walked to his car, wondering, *What the hell is going on with Sammie?*

When he got to the hospital, he asked for Samantha Marcs' room at the front desk. Before the receptionist could take his information and give him a visitor's sticker, Dr. Desmond approached him.

"Are you Mr. Malik Marcs?" she asked, seeming all too anxious to meet him.

"Yes. Is my wife okay?" he asked with concern etched in his voice.

"She's stable now. Follow me," she said as she led him down the hall. "She was feeling a little lightheaded. We're giving her intravenous fluids."

"Lightheaded?"

"Yes. We were meeting about the investigation, and she passed out on her way to the restroom. They're running bloodwork now." As Malik walks up to the door to the room where his wife was, Dr. Desmond walked off to give them privacy.

Malik walked over to the bed where Sammie was laying and rubbed her hair. She opened her eyes. "Hi," she whispered.

"Why are you at the hospital?" Malik asks.

"I didn't want to tell you until after everything was confirmed."

"Tell me what?"

Sammie motioned toward the chair in the corner that was holding the file that Dr. Desmond provided to her. "Can you hand me that paperwork?" she asked Malik.

He stepped over and grabbed it for her.

"Open it," she stated.

Malik looked through the material. "So…"

"So, you were poisoned—not by a drug but by a fruit. Unripe ackee fruit native to Jamaica."

Malik put the file down and stared off into the distance. "What? So, Casey really tried to…" Malik shook his head. A tear rolled down his cheek, not because he was sad but because he was becoming enraged with anger. Malik threw the paperwork down on the bed then paced the room. He stayed posted at the window for several seconds before turning around with a blank expression and more tears. "Samantha, I am so sorry." Before he could fully say the last word, he was crying uncontrollably at her bedside with his head on Samantha's stomach.

Samantha rubbed his head and allowed him to release. As she was with him in this moment, she thought, *This is exactly what we needed, a cleansing.* She thought about all of the anger she felt in regards to the cheating and lying, and a part of her thought she wouldn't get past it and that Malik wouldn't completely confess. The trust issues with her husband had already began to take hold of the relationship. She questioned his every move and started to wonder if she was enough for him. Most of all, she wondered if he would accept his responsibility in this mess so they could get past it.

Malik lifted his face up, wiping his tears away. "Samantha, I know I don't deserve a second chance, but if you could find it in your heart to forgive me...I promise to honor what we have going forward."

Samantha was silent.

Dr. Desmond cleared her throat to make it known she had just entered the room. "I'm sorry to interrupt," she said as she walked over toward Sammie and Malik. "You tested negative for any type of poisoning. We ran the same test we ran on your husband for the Jamaican vomiting disease.

"Well, that's a relief," Sammie said.

"Yes, it is," the doctor said as she thumbed through the iPad. "There is something," she said and looked up at the couple.

Sammie and Malik waited on her "something," wondering what it could be.

"Mrs. Marcs, you're pregnant."

"What?" she and Malik asked in unison.

"I take it you didn't know."

"Well, we had been trying but..." Samantha managed to get out.

Malik laughed, "Baby, we're pregnant," he stated gingerly, then lowered his face to her belly and kissed it.

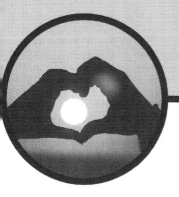

CHAPTER 14

WILLIAM'S SEXY NIGHT

William woke up to Sara in his arms. It was just like old times. The sex was out of this world with her, but when he kissed her lips last night, why did he imagine it was Sabine's lips he was touching? When he turned her around and looked in her eyes after doing her from behind because it is her favorite position, he wondered how Sabine would like it. How would he handle her in this type of setting—the room dimmed, the only lights visible were the candles, which were placed strategically all over on the dressers and the nightstands.

William thinks, *What if Sabine was naked in my bed—totally vulnerable to me? Me being inside of her, the closest I could be to a person. After banging her hard and fast from behind, I'd soften my touch as I turned her around and swiped a piece of hair from her face. Her mouth would open as she takes deep breaths trying to recover. I'd plant soft sweet kisses on both cheeks then her lips again. Massaging her breasts softly at the base and working my way up to her nipples watching them as they become hard and erect, like little erasers. I'd put my mouth to one nipple then the other. She would moan softly. My dominate hand would slide down to her sex and begin fingering her. She'd be so wet, which is how I could tell she enjoyed the sex, but I wouldn't be done. I'd have more angles to hit inside of her warm, velvet walls. I'd want to hear her scream and yell out my name at least two more times before the night was over.*

As William reflected on his night with Sara, he realized he really preferred to be making love to Sabine. He considered all of the thoughts running through his mind...

He continued his dialoged with himself in his thoughts, feeling conflicted, *I'm very fond of Sara. It's like we are kindred spirits, but I'm so curious about Sabine. There's so much potential there for us. I wonder if she ever thinks of me as more than just a friend. We joke all the time with a sexual undertone, but is she just humoring me, or are there feelings she's covering up? Maybe I need to sit down and have a heart to heart with her about marrying Kelvin. She's only known him for a few months and only a few weeks longer than she's known me. Kelvin is always on the road, and she and I are always hanging out together. I make her laugh. She's herself around me. She needs someone who can be there for her every day, not someone who's out of town every other week "on business." For all she knows, Kelvin could be cheating on her. She's so trusting. He could have a double life with another woman in one of the states he travels to often. I know Sabine feels the energy and chemistry we have. Of course, right now, it's all dormant, potential energy due to our position with each other. And by position I mean Kelvin being positioned between what could potentially be between Sabine and me. I respect her situation with Kelvin of course. Kelvin is one lucky bastard.*

Sara turned to face William in the bed. "What's on your mind?" she asked.

"Nothing. Just thinking about this case with Casey."

"Okay, so I know you didn't call me up last night just for sex. What do you want to know about Casey?"

"Last night you were telling me a story about Montego Bay..."

"Yeah." Sara sat up and pulled her hair up and held it in place. Let me wash my face and maybe we can discuss it over breakfast," she said and she got out of the bed.

BREAKFAST AT THE CAFÉ

WILLIAM

Sara and William walked through the doors of S & S Café and had a seat at a round intimate table in the corner. Immediately they were greeted by Lamar, the waiter. "Good morning, Mr. Witford," he said to William and nodded at William's guest, then handed them both a paper menu with today's special and an array of different teas and coffee.

"Good morning, Lamar," William said, looking around the café in search of Sabine.

"Ms. Stallworth is upstairs with clients. She's booked all day," Lamar said as he watched William search the room with no success then focus his attention on the menu. "Today's special consists of an omelet of your choice, a side of toast, and your choice of drink. If you don't want the special, you can choose between pancakes or waffles with a side of turkey bacon or sausage, or any pastry we have in the display."

Sara spoke up. "Thank you, Lamar. I'll have a Danish and a cup of coffee—black with sugar." Sara handed Lamar the menu. "I'm Sara, by the way," she said to him and extended her hand out to shake his.

He quickly grabbed the menu and shook Sara's hand. "Nice to meet you," he said then angled his body in William's direction.

"I'll have the omelet with sausage and cheese and a tall glass of apple juice." William handed Lamar the menu.

"Thank you. Your order will be up in a few," Lamar said as he walked away.

"Sara, last night at the bar you were telling me about the two guys in Montego Bay with Casey."

"Yes. So, she met up with two guys—one of Haitian descent and the other of Cambodian descent—one evening. They came to our hotel room. It was the strangest thing I've ever experienced, partly because they were speaking in French at times. But, I remember they had this book they were working out of that had symbols like hieroglyphics etched on the pages. They were teaching her a chant and showing her different things that resembled animal parts. She would recite chants over and over until it looked as if her eyes were rolling into the back of her head. Her body seemed to relax," Sara said, recalling the memory. "Eventually, I drifted off to sleep. I woke up a few hours later. Everything seemed different from the sound of the ocean from our balcony to the music that was playing in the background. When I got up to look for her, there was smoke all throughout the room, and I was in a haze. I heard the man's voice who was of Cambodian descent as though it was in my head." Sara stopped her story and looked at William. "I admit I was in an altered state due to the wine I had been drinking earlier that day and other recreational activities I had engaged in, but I was fully aware of what was going on. It was like being in a dream state but awake, if that makes sense."

Lamar walked over and put the meals and drinks on the table, then asked, "Do you need anything else right now?"

William responded, "No. We're good for now. Later, I would like to speak to you about the email you sent me."

Lamar nodded. "I'll be back over to check on you in a few."

Sara opened sugar packets, poured them into her coffee, and stirred, then took a bite of her Danish, and wiped her mouth with a napkin.

William sliced into his omelet and took a bite then said, "What was the Cambodian man saying to you?"

"He was whispering to me in another language, but I couldn't find him in the room. I couldn't find Casey or the Haitian man either. I went outside and laid in one of the beach chairs near the ocean. It was dark. I guess I drifted back off to sleep. I woke up to the sound of Casey crying. She was a few feet away from me and laying in the sand."

William continued to devour his omelet and waited on Sara to finish the story.

"I walked over to her. She seem visibly okay. But, she sobbed for hours. I just sat with her and held her. The next day, she couldn't recall the guys coming to the room or anything that happened after, but her personality became more estranged. She was to herself more. She'd seem to have conversations referring to herself in third person. At first I thought those guys gave her a bad fix, but this lasted for months."

William nodded and continued to listen intently and eat.

"I felt nervous around her—uncomfortable. She didn't feel like the same girl after our trip. Almost like..." Sara paused, unsure if she should say what she was thinking.

"Almost like what?" William stopped eating and looked at Sara.

"Nothing."

"Sara, tell me."

"I don't know, like she brought something back with her. Like something latched itself to her and was cooperating with her body."

"Oh," William said.

"Then she started to sabotage my friendships with people— high school stuff, like starting rumors and other silly things I can't really remember. Any guy I would try to pursue, she would win them over, and they'd seem to be very enticed by her." She raised her eyebrow to William.

William shifted in his seat.

"I moved out of the dormitory, then our friendship just fell off. That's when I met you. Everything was all good, until now."

"Why did you never tell me this? I mean we dated for years," William asked.

"Sometimes things leave a bad taste in your mouth and you just want to move past it. Sometimes revisiting it opens it back up. I'm telling you now because you asked, and I want to help you with this case. I think it would give closure to our relationship."

"What?" William questioned.

"I mean me and Casey's relationship."

William thought back to how he and Sara met during his last few months in law school. How when he saw her walking across his path, he immediately was drawn to her. He pretended she dropped her pen and returned it to her. She was in such a rush she didn't know if she dropped the pen or not. She barely looked at him when she thanked him. Because William had been working at his father's firm, he reached in his wallet and pulled out the business card that read *Witford & Associates* and handed it to her, then he said, "If you really want to thank me, call me after class and let me take you to lunch." She ran off to class.

After the first date, it felt like they knew each other all of their lives.

William graduated law school that year, and Sara graduated one year later. They were a match made in heaven—until Casey ran into William at court one day and asked him out. It wasn't his intension to cheat on Sara. There was something about Casey that was enticing and mesmerizing. Not that Casey's looks superseded Sara's nor were her wits or intelligence more than Sara's. There was something about Casey that night at dinner that lured him, for lack of better words. And it kept him coming back—canceling dates with Sara just to see Casey.

Sara shook William's hand across the small table. "William," she questioned, "are you okay?"

"Yes." William put his fork down. "I'm sorry, I was just... thinking about when we first met."

Sara smiled. "Well, I need to go. I have an appointment."

"With who?" William asked without thinking.

"Mr. Witford, you lost your rights to that information months ago," she said with her right eyebrow raised. "Thank you for last night though, and for breakfast. Call me later." Sara walked over to William, kissed him on the cheek and exited the café.

Shortly after, Sabine walked over to William's table, lightly rubbed his shoulder and had a seat in Sara's chair.

"Hi. You okay?" she asked.

William smiled, feeling comforted just by Sabine's presence. Thinking of the past and how everything went wrong in his relationship with Sara, opened up a wound that wasn't fully healed. "Yes, love. Now that you're here," he said, staring lovingly at Sabine.

"Who was the special lady you were eating breakfast with?" Sabine asked.

William turned to look at the door. "Oh, that was Sara."

"The...Sara?"

"Yes." William said. "I wanted you to meet her, but Lamar said you were busy counseling clients upstairs."

"Yes. It's a busy day. I'm exhausted, William. Tomorrow I'll get to rest." Sabine looked over to see her next client enter. "I've gotta go. Call me later." She walked over to a frail woman who looked very shy and escorted her upstairs to her office.

CHAPTER 16

THE ENTANGLED UNIVERSE

SABINE

Sabine rushed out of the café at seven p.m. after finishing up with her last counseling client for the day. *Today was jam-packed*, she thought. She looked for her keys to lock the café door. Sabine's cell phone rang, and she picked up.

"Hi, baby." Sabine relayed love and sincerity across the phone by the tone in her voice when she noticed it was Kelvin calling.

"Hi, sweetie. How was your day?"

"Busy, but good. How was yours?" Sabine asked.

"Eventful. I got another account. I'll tell you all about it later tonight. I should be home by eleven."

"Okay. I love you, Kelvin, but I've gotta go," Sabine said as she found her keys, picked her purse up off the table, turned out the lights, and head toward the door.

"Love you too, sweetie. Where are you going?" he asked.

"I'm just leaving work. I have an appointment with Amanda, the lady we met at Club Enticement."

"Really? In regards to what?" Kelvin asked suspiciously.

"I'll tell you later, when I get home. See you tonight. I was looking for the keys to the café's front door, I found them, but I don't have my ear buds, and I'm about to lock up and get in the car."

"Okay. Drive safe. Talk to you later," Kelvin said reluctantly.

Sabine jumped into her car and headed toward the back roads following the directions Amanda had given her last time via text. Most of what she wrote were landmarks on where to turn, but it was very specific—*go around the winding curve for about a mile and a half until you see a dilapidated barn, then veer right at the yield sign.* Sabine most definitely appreciated Amanda's attention to detail, especially so late in the evening. Everything looked different at night. As Sabine was rounding the curve, a deer passed over the road. She stopped suddenly to avoid hitting the animal, which caused her to swerve off the road into a ditch. *Oh my God,* she thought as she assessed the situation, making sure she was okay. She opened her car door and exited. Using the flashlight feature on her cell phone, she walked around the car checking the tires. The car was fine. Now, if she could just find a way to back up out of this ditch. As she was walking toward the street to get a better scope of the area, she felt that flickering in her mind that was starting to become all too familiar. It reminded her of back in the day, before cable, when she'd turn to a channel on a television, but the picture was fuzzy, she'd turn the knob delicately to find the right spot where you got reception. Well, it seemed as if she'd stepped in the right spot. She gained access to a consciousness not confined through space and time—those places beyond the surface reality, where all things were connected. Carl Jung, the Swiss psychiatrist who founded analytical psychology, termed it the collective unconscious.

Sabina see a dark road, like the one she's walking on now. She walks over to a barn and can hear a man moaning. When he comes into her sight, she realize he's older. He has a bruised eye, and there are blood stains on his shirt. As she walk past him around to the front of the barn, she see Amanda's house, but it looks different. There is a wraparound porch, but her little white table isn't there. In fact, the house seems abandoned. It's nighttime, but there are no lights on in the house or on the porch. As Sabine gaze back over at the barn, she sees a figure walking with a lantern heading in the direction she just left the older gentleman. As she is making her way back over, a pickup truck pulls off. She look down where she left the old man. No one's there.

A horn honks, and Sabine realize in her dimensional slippage, or reality shift, she wander further up the road. She don't see her car anymore. The car pulled up beside her. It was Amanda.

"Sweetheart, are you okay?" she asked.

"My car veered off into a ditch."

"Get in. We'll go back to my house and call a tow truck," she said.

When they reached Amanda's home, the porch was lit and there were lights on inside. Sabine looked off to the side where she saw the barn in her vision, but it was just plowed land.

As if Amanda could sense Sabine was looking for something she said, "There used to be a barn there. I had it torn down. A lot a bad memories. I plant tomatoes, greens, and onions there now."

Once inside, they took a seat at Amanda's kitchen table. "It's so spacious yet cozy in here," Sabine said.

"Thank you, darling. Do you want to use my house phone to call the tow truck?" she asked.

"No. I'll use my cell phone, I have AAA. Let me call them now."

Amanda prepared green tea with lemon.

After Sabine was done with the phone call, she took a sip of the tea. "How did you know to come looking for me?"

"You were thirty minutes late and your phone kept going to voice mail. It's dark, and I know these roads can be tricky."

Sabine nodded and sipped more of her tea, still trying to decipher the vision she saw.

"And...I tuned into you, Sabine. I could see you were in and out of different worlds—what I term vertical dreaming."

"What?" Sabine asked.

"This is why I wanted you to come see me in the first place. Your skills are advancing, and I need to help you hone them—help you get a grip so you don't hurt yourself."

Sabine took a deep breath.

"You've learned how to time travel, mostly to the past. It's like lucid dreams, portals to other worlds."

"Like parallel universes?"

"Yes, exactly," She exclaimed happily. "We live in an interactive universe. We're in one of the many worlds out there. Science always talk about time travel, thinking we need a machine, like in that movie *Back to the Future,* but time travel is available as a mental vehicle. Does that make sense?"

"It does," Sabine replied.

"You're very advanced in your clairs; clairvoyance, clairaudience, clairsentience, and you have empathic abilities. You can pick up on people's feelings and emotions without them being verbally expressed, this is what makes you a great counselor. You know how people feel without them expressing it verbally. But, I need to teach you how to navigate within this 'entangled universe.' Before we begin, do you have any questions for me?"

"Yes, in the vision I had before you picked me up, you saw what I saw, right?"

"Yes."

"Who was the man with the lantern walking around the barn?"

"Sweetheart, maybe we should wait until I—"

"Please, I want to know," Sabine replied.

Amanda took a deep breath, then said, "It was your father."

After a few seconds have passed by, Sabine asked, "Why was daddy out there?"

"I told you I knew your parents. Your mom, Naomi Ruth, was friends with my mom, Nadine Johnson. Your father was sort of my protector after my mother passed away. My mom's husband was my stepfather. She had me before they were married. I never met my real dad, but that night, I found out who he was."

"Did my dad hurt that old man?"

"That old man was my stepfather. He wasn't himself that night. Your dad protected me from him."

CHAPTER 17

SESSION WITH AMANDA

SABINE

Sabine sat at Amanda's table shocked by this new revelation in regards to her dad and Amanda's stepfather, now understanding why Amanda felt it wasn't the best time to explore this vision. *I need to get a grip*, Sabine thinks. Sabine was having less and less control of her vertical dreaming as Amanda termed it. Things seemed to be triggered by location now. Just being in the area where things took place years ago, seemed to open up a vortex of insight and knowledge for her. Sabine questioned to herself, *Why? How was that relevant to me in this current place and time?*

Amanda broke Sabine's silence, thinking, and tea drinking by asking, "How long did the tow company say it would take?"

"Umm, about an hour," she replied.

"Okay, so we have an hour together today," Amanda responded. "I figured we'd start with the hows and the whys of the reason your ability has been amped up over the past few months." She walked back over to the kitchen table after refilling both teacups and placed the kettle back on the stove. "So the gentleman who was with you at the club when we first met each other, how's the relationship going between you two?"

"Kelvin?" Sabine asked.

"Yes, Kelvin," she said as she took a seat in front of her.

"We're engaged." Sabine showed Amanda the ring.

Amanda took her hand and admired the heart-shaped diamond wrapped in white gold, "Very nice."

"My relationship with him is different from anything I've ever experienced." As Sabine said this, she thought about the progression of Kelvin and her relationship over the past few months. Things seemed to have developed quickly from their first date to moving in together. "He's on the road a lot, gone almost every other week for days at a time to Michigan, Ohio, Illinois, Florida you name it. He's opening up new accounts and expanding on his logistics business. But the love is strong— yet there is really no rhyme or reason. If I tried to dissect and understand our connection logically, it doesn't really make sense. From the first day I met him, I swear, I loved him. It felt like we had met before or like it was a continuation of something. There was something familiar about him that felt like home."

Amanda smiled and sipped her tea as she listened to Sabine ramble about Kelvin, "Perfect, sweetie! Just perfect," she said.

Sabine chuckled and blushed about her long admission on her feelings for her fiancé.

"I would expect no less. He is indeed your twin flame."

"My what?"

"Your twin flame," she replied simply as if Sabine should know what she was referring to. "The purpose of a twin flame is to raise the vibrational frequency. Kelvin is your mirror—he has come to you to show you all of your unhealed parts and vice versa. You two will heal together. When you met Kelvin, it started your spiritual awakening. Have you noticed the telepathic connection going on between the two of you?"

"Yes," Sabine replied, thinking of the countless times Kelvin read her mind, tapped into her visions, and the visions she'd had in regards to him. It was all so overwhelming. He seemed to read into situations with ease.

"He's a little more evolved than you spiritually, but your natural abilities have been amplified, mostly in your dreams, and your ability to pick up on how others are feeling, and more recently, events of the past," Amanda said.

"Yes. I feel like I'm living in an alternate universe sometimes. I mean, I love what I have with Kelvin. It's like all my dreams are coming true in regards to having someone in my life who I love and who loves me back, but I can't shake the feeling that maybe he's hiding something from me. My suspicion lies in the fact that he's on the road more than he is at home. We had this incident before we were engaged, where I caught him making out with another woman…well, more like I energetically picked up on it. With Kelvin, I acquired something wonderful and beautiful, but it came with some flaws," Sabine confessed.

"Yes. I know. The connection you two share is rare. The average person on the outside looking in wouldn't understand. But you see, the connection you have isn't as simple as it would seem. There are challenges to overcome. The question you should ask yourself is, 'What is the meaning behind the relationship between you and Kelvin?' It doesn't matter how you started, sweetie. What's the meaning behind it?"

Amanda stressed the phrase *meaning behind it.*

"You see, there's no start or end point, no right or wrong. It's just perspective, and it's a cycle of life between you two. What does Kelvin mean to you? Let's start there."

Sabine shook her head, really trying to fully understand what Amanda was asking of her, but her thoughts felt flighty, and her mind was scattered. On one end, she wanted this magical fairy-tale ending, but how could she get this ending when she hadn't filled in the middle parts? She thought, *All the stories told to me as a young girl about love, about how Cinderella met her Prince Charming. It worked up to the part about how the prince won over the princess' love and vice versa, but then it skipped to living happily ever after. No one ever went into detail between the dating and marriage phases and thereafter. Isn't there a Cinderella part two, that shows what to do and how to feel at this point in the story, which is my life?*

"I feel a lot of emotions toward Kelvin. Some things I don't understand in regards to him, which leaves me feeling baffled.

I can understand so much about other people; a random person walking down the street, or in my counseling chair, but with Kelvin it's different. We tune into each other without even trying, and it causes a lot of conflict between us because of it. When he's in a good mood, my mood is not so good, but not because of anything he's done. It's just that our moods always seem opposite of each other. That's why I like the dating phase, when you are having a bad day, you just don't come around. But when you're having a bad day and you live with your spouse, what do you do, avoid them? Argue with them? Blame them? I can't help but think Kelvin is avoiding me."

"I can understand your frustration, Sabine. It's hard, but this is the cycle of any long-lasting relationship, especially for one that's as special as yours and Kelvin's. In this situation, you write the script. Those fairytales start at step one, the unexpected encounter of two souls and wraps up a multistep process into that one step. *Boom!* They fall in love. *Boom!* They face a challenge. *Boom!* They run away together against all odds. Part two of the story would be too real to be labeled fairytale. It's too real world to be placed in a fabricated storyline intended for young girls, giving them a false reality of life…you know, those little half-truths like Santa Claus and the Tooth Fairy."

Amanda paused for a minute, smiling.

"Sabine, there is no fairytale romance, and you're a grown woman. Real connections force you to deal with the deep-cleansing process a relationship brings. You two are both cleaning up the mess the ego unleased. All of those doubts and suspicious feelings in your mind started to increase for a reason. It's to bring up and break down all of those futile belief systems. All those old perceptions that you told yourself about life and love. The part two of the fairytale story is left unscripted for a reason…that's where the life lessons are, and that's where all the magic is."

Just as Amanda finished her statement, the tow company called to get the exact location of the vehicle. Amanda drove Sabine to her car. On the drive over, she explained that Kelvin and Sabine's meeting was an activation of some sort—that there union is meant to bring about change. Change is uncomfortable, but it served a purpose to help people elevate to their highest level of self, self-actualization. She said before Kelvin and Sabine were born, they agreed when they crossed paths, they would wake each other up, so to speak, that they made a promise to never let each other be less than what they truly are. She said Kelvin and Sabine's purpose, their *soul* purpose, was to evolve spiritually, and they could only be happy once the heart is broken a little.

"I'm going to show you a little trick that will help you and Kelvin's relationship. Just remember, you don't have to figure everything out in one night. It's a process, Sabine. Embrace the process."

There was no cost in relation to the towing company pulling Sabine out of the ditch. There was also no damage to the car. Sabine checked her voicemail messages as she was driving back home. She got a message from Jane, the wedding planner:

"Sabine, this is Jane Smith. I am the wedding planner assigned to you. Call me so we can figure out a good time to meet up to map out the blueprints to your wedding. I'm really looking forward to working with you and Kelvin. My number is 255-6403. Talk to you soon. Bye."

Just as she pushed seven to save the message and go to the next, William called, and she clicked over.

"Hello, William."

"Hi, love. Did I catch you at a bad time?" he asked.

"No. Perfect timing actually. I'm driving home."

"You were not still at work, were you?" he asked.

"No. I just left a friend's house. What's up?"

"I just met with Lamar."

"And...?"

"Why don't you let me take him off your hands and hire him at the firm as a paralegal and research specialist?"

"Um, no."

"He's on top of his shit. Do you know he wrote a report to

me detailing things I asked for and with perfect formatting and references? If I could use him as an expert witness, I would."

"I hope you're paying him well and not just using him."

"Yes, yes, he's been well compensated. I would never use anyone, Sabine. It's not who I am."

"I know. I'm sorry I even said that." Sabine paused for a minute as she allowed her self to come down from her session with Amanda, then refocused to her current conversation with William, "So, Sara, huh?"

"Yup, Sara."

"You guys have fun reigniting your passion?" Sabine joked.

William was uneasy. Sabine could feel it across the phone. He didn't respond.

"William, I was just playing around. We don't have to talk about that if you don't want to."

"No, it's not that," he murmured. "She's helping me get some background knowledge on Casey. They were college roommates, and I contacted her for research purposes."

"Okay. Was she able to help?"

"Yes. We need to get together to discuss things. I've been stopping by the salon, and Casey's not there anymore, according to the staff who works there. It looks like she was working under someone else's name. They hired her as the manager of that location, but let her personalize the building with her name. But now that she has a pending case, the original owners are taking it back over."

"Well, that's good news. When exactly is the court date?" Sabine asked.

"At the beginning of the new year. It's been the focus of most of my work these days. Your sister reached out to me and would like for me to take Malik's case."

CHAPTER 18

SUNDAY DINNER

SABINE

Samantha and Malik walked into the house more chipper than Sabine's seen them in months. They've brought drinks, she could tell by the bags they were holding.

"Hey, girl," Samantha said as Sabine hugged her. "It's time to celebrate the first full successful week of the café opening. We'll discuss the numbers later, but for now all I have to say is that it's all good."

Sabine smiled and looked at Malik with eyes full of curiosity, then hugged him. He said, "Hi sis." He was smiling ear to ear.

"Okay, what's the good news?" Sabine asked, looking between the two of them.

"Is Kelvin here?" Malik asked.

Yes. He's on the patio out back setting up the table. He grilled," Sabine replied.

"We'll make the announcement once dinner starts," Samantha exclaimed. She went into the kitchen and put a few sodas in the refrigerator, then two sparkling grape juices. Malik walked outside to the patio to greet Kelvin.

"No wine?" Sabine asked Samantha.

"Sabine, I'm pregnant," Samantha blurted.

"What?" Sabine screamed, jumping up and down.

"*Shh.* I told Malik we'd make the announcement together."

"Oh my goodness, girl. How long have you known?"

"It was by accident that I found out. Remember I had that appointment with Dr. Desmond on Thursday?"

"Yes," Sabine replied.

"I fainted during the appointment. At first I thought I was just overwhelmed by the whole ordeal with Casey. They confirmed Malik was poisoned with ackee fruit at the club that night. I was feeling light headed and nauseous after the news. I remember walking to the restroom, next thing I know...I was in a hospital bed."

Malik walked into the kitchen. "Kelvin's done grilling, and I'm ready to eat!"

Samantha and Sabine walked out of the kitchen with a bottle of juice, a bowl of ice, and the decanter to pour it in.

"I love the decorations," Sammie said as she looked around to see the screened-in porch decorated with inside lights which reminded her of Christmas. The table was set formally with corn on the cob, broccoli, fresh fruit, and potato salad in the center. Kelvin walked up and placed a plate full of grilled chicken, ribs, and sausage on the table.

"Thanks. I wanted to do something special. I think we should start back eating dinner together as a family, like we did when Mom and Dad were alive, in honor of their memory and to make new memories in continuing the legacy," Sabine said.

"Let's say grace," Kelvin said as he reached for their hands.

Sammie and Sabine reached for Malik's hands.

"Thank you for bringing us together as family today, Father God. We pray for continued gatherings filled with love and happiness. We would like to extend our gratitude for the successful launch of S&S Café and Lounge. Continue to protect and bless this family and our union between You, Universal Source. Whatever our purpose is this lifetime, I pray we fulfill it with peace, love, and light. Amen."

"Amen," everyone repeated.

"Sabine, why do you have two extra place mats set?" Samantha asked, referring to the seats that were saved for William and Sara.

"Because we're expecting two more." As soon as Sabine said this, the doorbell rang. "That's them right now. Excuse me."

Kelvin, Malik and Samantha looked around at each other, all questioning who the guests might be. Sabine walked back into the room seconds later. "Everyone, you all know William."

"Good evening, good people. Nice to see everyone again," William said. "This is Sara Mansfield, my date for tonight."

Sammie stood and walked over to hug William and his date, then said, "Come sit over here." William shook hands with Kelvin and Malik, then sat down.

"We've already blessed the food. We were just about to dig in," Kelvin said and took a bite of the corn.

As everyone has filled their plates with food, Sammie stood up and hits her glass with a fork. She grabbed Malik's arm and tugged at him to stand with her. Malik held a piece of grilled chicken in his hand and was smiling ear to ear. Sammie said, "We have an announcement to make," she paused and looked around the table and then back at Malik, grabbing his free hand, "Malik and I are three months pregnant!"

"Wow! Congratulations!" William said as he stood and hugged her, which was followed by hugs from everyone at the table. Samantha's announcement set the tone for a festive evening filled with celebration.

Dinner was coming to an end. Sabine sat around the table looking at her family with gratitude. She thought to herself, *Sammie and I successfully launched our café and lounge, Kelvin was effectively managing Frey Transportation, Inc. both here in Florida and in Michigan, and William was managing the law firm his father passed on to him. This is the meaning of dreams coming true. To add to it all, Samantha and Malik are having a baby, which has been something Malik has wanted since the beginning of their marriage.*

Even though Sabine sat to the table with family feeling content with everyone around, she started to remember how it felt when her mom and dad were alive and eating family dinner with them. She began to feel a little emotional. She looked over at Kelvin and he winked his eye at her and smiled a seductive smile. As he sat back in his chair his phone rang.

Kelvin answered, "Hello, Frey Transportation!" He paused and looked toward Sabine, then whispered, "I gotta go take this call. I need to go into the office for a little while, I'll be back shortly. Can you let them know," he said gesturing at their guests.

Sabine nodded her head.

Kelvin kissed her on the forehead and walked into the kitchen from the patio and then he was out of sight.

Sabine looked over to William and Sara and thought, *Sara is beautiful.* She admired her yellow toned skin, naturally curly black hair, thick full lips, and beautifully vibrant grey eyes. William's eyes met with Sabine's a few seconds. His smile left his face, and concern was in his eyes. Then she looked over at her sister and Malik, who were laughing and thinking of baby names. Malik was coming up with all kinds of crazy names, and Sammie was looking at Sabine like, "Is he serious?" Sabine smiled at them, then excused herself from the table, taking a few of the empty plates with her.

As she was in the kitchen, she placed a few dishes into the washer. William walked in and over to her.

"Sabine, are you okay?" he asked.

"Yes. Did you enjoy dinner?" she asked, sort of brushing off the question.

He stood near her and grabbed her hand. "Dinner was great. Listen, love, I've known you long enough to be able to tell if there's something wrong with you. Something's on your mind. Talk to me."

I'm overwhelmed, sad, and wondering if this is where I am supposed to be, she thought. *I feel alone. Even though I'm in this relationship with Kelvin, he's hardly ever home, and when he is here, he seems absent emotionally. Something's missing.* "I just have a lot on my mind in regards to the business and stuff like that," Sabine rambled, cowering out on expressing her real feelings.

William looked her in the eyes, then said, "Can you break away from the café for a couple of hours for lunch tomorrow?"

She thought for a little while, then said, "Sure, I can do that. Eleven good for you?"

"It's perfect. Everything is going to be fine."

Sabine looked at William.

"With the café," he added.

"Yes," she responded, nodding. She untwined her fingers from his and continued to load the dishwasher with his help.

Kelvin walked in moments later with his work duffle bag on his shoulder.

"William, we have plenty of leftovers if you want to take some to go," he said as he pulled out containers from the cabinet to place the food into.

Sabine walked over toward Kelvin. "I'll do that, sweetie," she said to him.

"You sure?" he asked, trying to get a read on her mood.

"Yes, if you need to go in to work, I got this."

Kelvin reached over to embrace her. He held her for seconds, then exited the kitchen and their home after kissing her once more.

William cleared his throat to remind Sabine that he was still in the kitchen. When she turned to face him, tears were streaming down her cheeks. She wiped them with the palm of her hand then excused herself to the bathroom.

CHAPTER 19

LOVERS' SPAT

SABINE

After Sabine's nightly bedtime routine, she walked out into the living room to check the patio and front door to make sure they were locked. She walked over to a shelf and looked at the photos of Kelvin and her together at the beach. One with Sabine in his lap, and him hugging her close, Sabine could practically feel the happiness on that day as if it was happening right now.

Sabine thinks to herself, *I'm afraid of how out of control I feel in relation to my feelings for him. We haven't started planning the wedding yet.* She called the wedding planner back and left a message, and the wedding planner left a message on her voicemail asking for the best time to meet. Sabine haven't even asked Kelvin for a date that works for him, so they can meet Mrs. Smith for the first time together. Just as Sabine turned to walk over to flip the light switch off, Kelvin walks over to her.

"Did you enjoy Sunday dinner, baby?" he asked.

"I didn't hear you come in," Sabine said confused, then, "Yes. It was nice. Thank you for helping to make that happen."

He rubbed her shoulders then grabbed her hand and walked with her to the bedroom. Sabine walked over to her side of the bed and Kelvin to his.

"Sweetie, are you okay?" Kelvin asked.

She laid her head down softly on the pillow, reflecting on the question, then began to speak. "It's late. Did you take care of what you needed to with work?"

"Yes. I hope it was really okay with you that I had to leave," he says looking at her.

"What am I supposed to say, 'no, don't go?'" Sabine asked, then continued, not allowing him to respond, "What's your schedule like next week?"

"I'm going to be in Jacksonville Tuesday until the end of the week," Kelvin replied.

"Have you opened an office there?" she asked.

"No, but I should. I get a lot of business in that area." As Kelvin said this, he reached over and put his arms around Sabine's waist and pulled her in close to spoon. "Why didn't you tell me about your car going into a ditch yesterday?"

Sabine doesn't respond, feeling angered by his question but more upset that he is gone so much.

"I'm not invading your thoughts. The tow company works with Frey Transportation. I know the owner, and he was the one who came to tow your car out of the ditch."

Sabine remained silent.

"Sweetie, I'm not trying to..." Kelvin started to say then stopped midway and inhaled deeply.

"Not trying to what, Kelvin? Keep tabs on me?" she asked irritably.

"Wow," he said as he sat up and turned Sabine to face him. They stared at each other for a few minutes. Sabine could tell he was trying to get a read on her, but he couldn't. She'd effectively blocked him out, thanks to the technique Amanda showed her last night.

As the tow truck driver pulled her car out of the ditch, Sabine and Amanda stood there and watched and Amanda said, "Close your eyes, Sabine. I'm going to teach you something. Take a deep breath in, pulling in peace. Hold your breath for five, four, three, two, one seconds. Now let go. As you slowly release, imagine first a pink bubble surrounding your body like a globe. Now put a blue bubble around that bubble. Hold the intent that the bubbles will only allow what you want to be allowed in or out of your energy field. This way, you aren't so transparent and Kelvin won't be able to read your thoughts so easily. This will help your relationship. Make him have to do the real work instead of taking the easy route. When you're in your counseling sessions and want to pick up on people's energy, let the blue bubble down only. I'll explain more later. Practice." Then she hugged Sabine, and Sabine got into her own car.

"I didn't tell you because it was no big deal. There was no damage to the car, and I was fine," Sabine rattled off, speaking in a condescending manner.

"I was just concerned, Sabine. When I got home last night you were asleep. We didn't get to talk," Kelvin said sincerely.

"Okay, well, had you not gone to the office this morning before I woke up, or this evening before dinner was completely over, we would have had that time to talk. When there's something to be concerned about, I'll be sure to give you a full report."

"Sweetie… What's—"

Before he could finish asking Sabine what's wrong, she lay back down and said, "Good night."

He sat up in the bed for a while, then reached over to turn his lamp off and laid down.

CHAPTER 20

LUNCH DATE

WILLIAM

William waited downstairs as Sabine finished up with her client. He ordered a black tea—warm—with honey and an apple crisp dessert. As Lamar bought his entree over to the table he asked, "How was the report that I provided to you, Mr. Witford?"

"Lamar, it provided me with every detail about the Obeah religion or cult practices I never wanted to know. It was broken down with the most accurate details and structured and organized perfectly. I told Sabine, if I could use you as an expert witness, I would. Thank you for that. I hope the compensation was enough," William said as he poured honey into his tea.

"Yes, it was more than enough. Thank you, sir. If you need my services again, I'm here." Lamar walked to the kitchen.

Sabine walked over toward William. "You ready? Even though I don't understand why we can't have lunch at the best café in town," she said with a half-smile.

William stood to hug her. They both sat down together. "I wouldn't want your future husband to walk in, see us eating together, and have a fit."

"Kelvin's cool with our friendship now, so . . ." Sabine trailed off.

"If he's smart, he should continue to be on his best behavior.

Sabine, I don't mean any disrespect, but the minute he messes up, I'm going to be right here to catch you as you're falling. You were supposed to be mine this lifetime. Kelvin, the lucky bastard, just happened to meet you first."

Sabine smiled and stared at him, almost as if she was taking what he was saying to heart. "Well, where are you taking me to eat? I have the rest of the day off."

"Oh, so I get more than two hours?" William asked, sitting up in his seat.

"Ha, William. Don't get any ideas. I just thought we could take our time and eat."

William swallowed the remaining tea, stuffed the last piece of apple crisp into his mouth, placed a ten-dollar bill on the table, stood, and reached for Sabine's hand.

William and Sabine arrived at their destination—a villa with a private entry. As they exited the car, William walked over to Sabine's side and opened her door. He took her hand and they walked out back to a dining room area. A young man came to seat them outside on the patio and handed them two menus.

"Can I start you off with something to drink?"

William gazed over the wine menu quickly. "I would like to order a bottle of Far Niente Cabernet 2013," he said to the waiter.

"Can we have two glasses of water, also?" Sabine asked.

"Sure. Take your time and look the menu over, and I'll be back with the wine and waters," the waiter said.

"William, that wine is way too expensive."

"It's fine, lady. Did you prefer something different, or are you okay with that selection?"

"I'm okay with it," she said shyly and looked down at the menu, studying it as if William was going to quiz her on it.

"Sabine, there are only three entrees on the menu. Are you going to tell me what's been bothering you lately or continue to scrutinize that menu?"

"I told you. The first week of having the business open is new to me. I just feel..." she said as she searched for the word. "I think that I feel overwhelmed."

"Okay. I can see that. Now, is it just the business or other things too?"

Sabine took a deep breath.

"Listen love, we're friends. I'm not trying to overstep my boundaries. I know you're with Kelvin. I really just want to support you, offer you a sounding board. I'll be as unbiased as I can, okay? Why were you crying yesterday after dinner?"

One arm folded across her belly, her hand gripping her side, the other hand was in her hair. Sabine twirled her loose curls with her fingers. "You know, it's hard being in the hot seat. Now I know how my clients feel trying to open up."

"Well, maybe my technique is rusty. I always felt very comfortable opening up to you during our sessions."

The waiter came back with the wine and waters. He opened the bottle of Cabernet and filled their glasses halfway then set the bottle on the table. "Have you decided on a dinner choice?"

William looked over at Sabine.

"Yes. I'll have entree number two—the grilled salmon with asparagus and mashed potatoes."

"And you, sir?" the waiter turned to William.

"The same, please."

"I'll be back shortly with your orders." He reached for their menus.

"I thought I would feel more complete at this juncture in my life," Sabine continued.

"Yeah?"

"Yes. I mean, I feel happy I've accomplished what I've accomplished, but I guess I never imagined how I would feel when the business was up and running, and the same goes for being engaged."

She took a sip of her wine.

"Kelvin is gone a lot, and there was that issue in Key West I thought I forgave him for... I still feel a little shaken by it. I question if Kelvin really loves me at times, or if I just fit into an idea of what he wants in a wife."

She paused and sipped more of her wine, staring out into the distance. Seconds went by, and it seemed as if Sabine was drifting into her thoughts.

"Why do you think Kelvin would ask you to marry him if he wasn't really ready?"

"Maybe it's a phase of life he feels he should be in right now. He's accomplished his goals with his career. Now he's ready to add on to the American dream—settle down, buy a house together, and have kids," Sabine said in a monotone voice.

"So, are you just having second thoughts about the engagement, or are you questioning his character when it comes to a committed relationship?"

"He's gone so much, and if the situation in Key West hadn't have happened, maybe, just maybe, I wouldn't be so on edge about his whereabouts."

The waiter brought bread and olive oil to their table.

As the waiter walked away, Sabine stared William in the eyes awaiting his response to her statement. William was at a loss for words because what he wanted to say was *You should be concerned about his actions at the Key West trip. What man takes a beautiful woman on a romantic getaway to make out with a complete stranger?* But instead he said, "I think you're just getting the jitters, love. Your mind is starting to play tricks on you."

She stared at William for several more seconds. *Why does she do that?* William thought.

"Jitters, huh?"

"More or less, yes," he said.

"Okay," she said as she nodded her head. "Thank you, William, for listening to me. I'm happy we're friends."

"Listen, love, I hope you don't think I'm downplaying your feelings. I'm just trying to help you see other possibilities before jumping to conclusions."

"But, why do I feel you aren't telling me the truth?" she asked.

William paused and rubbed his fingers through his hair, opened his mouth to speak then closed it. The waiter showed up with their dinner entrees. He placed their food in front of them then asked if they needed anything else before excusing himself from the table.

As William picked up his fork, Sabine touched his hand. "William, this is one of those moments I want the truth—the way you started to speak at the Halloween party to Kelvin."

"Sabine...I can't... I don't think voicing my opinion will help out in this matter right now," he pleaded.

"Why not? I need you to tell me the truth, William, please. If I ever needed direction and guidance, this is the moment right now," she rebutted.

William took a deep breath. "I know Kelvin loves you because you're easy to love. I know he admires you because you're deep, honest, insightful, beautiful, and so many other things...yet, I do question his loyalty to you the way you're questioning it right now. I don't think he's working hard enough to make you feel comfortable in the relationship. Sometimes, men get content. He put that ring on your finger, and I feel he feels he's locked you in. He took you off the market. I'm not saying he wouldn't have asked you to marry him later down the road, but after just a few months of knowing him...I don't know."

Sabine forked her salmon and put a peace in her mouth. William's cell phone rang, and without looking he silenced the phone.

"I think he wanted to cover his tracks and have a reason to exert control in certain situations," he said, feeling the flood gates open and all of the truth seemed to be pouring out of him. William paused and looked at Sabine, who was eating her salmon and starting to smile. "What?" William questioned.

"Nothing. Thank you for being honest. I appreciate it."

William took a bite of his salmon. "Are you okay with what I said?" he asked her.

"Yes. I appreciate you more than you know. It feels good to talk to someone about this. Talking to you is easy—easy like Sunday morning. Do you remember that song?" Sabine asked, changing the subject.

"Yes, by Westlife."

"So, how is the case going with Casey?" Sabine asked.

"Really good. I got the video footage from the club. They emailed the jpg file over to me today. I haven't looked at it yet, but according to where Sammie said she and Malik were located during the time where she thinks Casey slipped the ackee fruit into the drink, there was a camera."

"What? They're recording people in that club?" Sabine asked, shocked.

"Well, not exactly. They have cameras positioned at certain angles near exits and some hallways. But according to the owner, you can see some of the guests, depending on where they're positioned."

"William, you and Casey visited that club often. You aren't afraid that something could leak out?" Sabine asked.

"It wouldn't leak out. If it did, they would have a serious lawsuit on their hands, trust me," he responded.

CHAPTER 21

WILLIAM'S WORK

WILLIAM AND SARA

After dropping Sabine back off to her café, Sara called.

"Hey, lover. Are you busy?" she asked.

"Just headed home to do some research on the case."

"Do you need any help? I could drop by in a few hours, and we could order Chinese food. It would be like old times—us working together."

"Okay. What time should I expect you?"

"Six," she said.

"See you then, Sara."

As William pulled into his driveway, he pressed the little button that clipped to his sun visor to open the garage. He saw a figure in the corner of the garage that seemed to fade the closer he gets to it. He squinted, trying to make out what the figure could be. Then he accelerated up the driveway, hurrying to see if his eyes were deceiving him. The figure disappeared once he's completely inside the garage. William grabbed his briefcase, turned the ignition off, and closed the car door. He walked around the car looking in the corners of the garage for whatever it was he thought he just saw. Nothing.

He walked up the two steps that led into the laundry room, which led to the kitchen of his home, looked back out toward the garage, then pressed the button to lower the door of the garage. He set his briefcase down and untied his shoelaces and neatly placed them in the laundry room area. On the kitchen counter was a note from Mrs. Santos, the woman he'd hired to clean his house once a week.

Mr. Witford,

I left you a voicemail in regards to this issue, but upon my entering your home today, a young woman was trying to unlock your door with a key she said you provided to her. She said she had left some of her things in the house that needed to be collected. I didn't let her in, but I went to the spare bedroom upstairs to look for the items she said were hers. I told her I didn't find anything, but when I looked in the drawer, I found this.

—Ms. Santos.

William picked up a book entitled, *Voodoo Handbook and Cult Secrets.* He flipped through the pages then put it down and picked up another book and read the title on the front cover, *Old Love Charm Spells.* Lastly, he picked up a package that looked like herbs. On the package it read, *Snake Root.* William threw the two books and herbs to the floor with force, upset with himself for letting that crazy, deranged woman live with him for a period of time. *Casey, Casey, Casey,* he thought, shaking his head. *Love spells? Really?* He grabbed a grocery bag and shoved the two books and the package of herbs into it, tied it tightly, and opened the laundry room door. He walked out into the garage and set it on a shelf, fighting the urge the throw it in the trash can. *I may have some use for this shit for the case,* he thought.

This little incident was exactly what he needed to jump-start his work on the case. Samantha provided all of the documentation from Dr. Desmond in regards to the club poisoning of Malik Marks. He pulled the information out of his briefcase, took it out of the envelope, positioning the papers in three different stacks on his desk, sorted by the staples on the packets of paper. William pulled out his laptop and opened the jpg file from Club Enticement. The video came through a little fuzzy when it first started. It was in black and white and no sound was available. The clock at the top of the screen was running in minutes and seconds. He watched until exactly eleven minutes and eleven seconds before pausing the video to see a figure standing in the hallway who looked to be observing. He unpaused the scene and held his finger over the button, watching as the figure walked into the room disappearing from sight for about half a minute, then exiting the room. He paused the screen once again and zoomed in on the face of one of the figures.

Just as he started to zoom, William heard a noise out in the garage. He stood and walked out of his office on the main floor of his house, cutting through the dining room and through the kitchen. He opened the laundry room door, which he never locked and flipped on the light switch in the garage. He grabbed a baseball bat that was sitting off to the side of the garage and cautiously walked around the space investigating the situation. Nothing. He circled the car a few more times to make sure. He noticed the items he'd placed in the bag that belonged to Casey was no longer on the shelf. His phone rang in the house.

William slowly exited the garage looking around uneasily, then locked the laundry room door as he re-enters the house. When he reached the desk in the office where his cell phone was located, the phone stopped ringing. He looked through the call history and it read unknown caller. He pressed the call button anyway, but he got an automated message, "The feature code you entered is not working."

William put the phone down and took a stroll around his house, checking the doors and windows. He walked upstairs into his loft area to ensure everything was in place. When he walked into the guest room where Casey use to sleep, an uneasy feeling hit his chest and his gut, causing him to yell out in pain. He sat on the edge of the bed and looked at the closet door, which was cracked, and a yellow glow was emanating light into the darken room.

"What the fuc—" William said out loud to himself as he eased up off the bed clutching at his chest. He crept over to the closet door and pushed it open.

CHAPTER 22

SEXY NIGHT

SAMANTHA AND MALIK

Samantha reached over to grab Malik's hand and placed it over her flat belly. "It seems like I can feel the baby move. Do you think that's my imagination?" she asked.

Malik rolled on his side and held his hand steadily on her belly, humoring her. "I don't think it's too early. I think you can feel our baby moving."

Samantha smiled, sat up and straddled one leg around Malik's waist, looking him deep in the eyes, then lowered herself and planted a soft kiss on his lips. Malik groaned. Sammie hesitated, thinking about the affair with Casey, and moved to get off her husband. He grabbed her at the waist, stopping her from leaving, pulled her body down to his, flipped her over and asked, "Where were you going?" He didn't wait for a reply. He simply kissed her softly at first and then with more passion, deepening the caress.

They both quickly lifted up and took off their clothes. Sammie shut off the television and threw the remote on the nightstand then quickly got back in position on the bed, lying flat on her back and reaching for Malik. He slowly moved in between her thighs, pulling at her legs, sliding her down closer near the edge of the mattress, then he lowered himself and reached out to grip her breasts, one then the other. Samantha's eyes were closed, and soft moans were escaping her lips. Malik kissed her neck while simultaneously massaging her nipples.

"Malik, I miss your touch," Sammie whispered as she gripped around his broad shoulders, enjoying the way he flicked his tongue on her neck, and the way the suctions of kisses felt as he trailed down toward her nipples. Sammie arched upward, needing to feel the pressure of his penis inside of her. The longing was becoming unbearable. She moaned and began rotating her hips upward trying to meet the head of his penis at her opening. As soon as the tip of his penis touched her clit, Malik began to gyrate, adding more and more pressure to her sensitive spot. He glided in slowly as they both let out a long, low gasp. He held his body to hers in that position for a few seconds, enjoying the sensation and her reactions. They both opened their eyes and stared lovingly at each other. Sammie reached up and grabbed Malik at his neck, pulling his face to her, and they commenced to kiss—deeply, passionately. Malik grinded hard and slow into her, keeping a steady pace for both of their enjoyment.

He whispered in her ear, "Sammie, I'm going to change up the tempo a little—if that's okay with you."

Samantha just moaned.

He scooped her up from the bed and stood with his wife wrapped around him. Using his upper-body strength, he lifted her up and down on his penis, speeding up the pace, straddling his legs wider, bending at the knees, and swerving his hips. His thrust went deeper and deeper until he could feel his wife's body contracting around his engorged man part.

Samantha yelled out in pleasure as Malik kissed her softly, slowing his motions almost to a complete stop. He walked her over to the bed, lay her down and asked, "Can you turn over and lay on your belly?"

Sammie complied.

He lay behind her, her butt cheeks pressing against his pelvis. He used his hand to insert his penis into her vagina from behind. He pulled her hips up a little and pulled back and slowly entered her.

Her breathing was heavy, and she anticipated his next move.

He made love to his wife slowly from behind until he could feel her cumming around his rock-hard penis again. The sound of her moans and the contractions of her body almost sent him over the edge, but he controlled it. He didn't want to cum right now. He wanted her to enjoy him longer. He wanted to love her harder, to show how much he adored and appreciated her.

He rolled over to his back, still inside of her, using his hips to thrust in and out at a fast pace. Her sweet juices were running down his penis. She reached down and rubbed his scrotum softly, caressing each testicle. They were no longer hanging away from his body, but drawn up tightly. He was close to cumming. Sammie squeezed her pelvic muscles from the inside, causing Malik to yell out in pleasure. He paused, trying to stop the orgasm that had already started spiraling.

"Sammie, you feel so good," he whispered softly in her ear.

Her attempt to make him cum, feeling his body almost release, and the idea that he wanted to pleasure her so much tonight set her off again.

"Malik," she panted, as if her body couldn't take anymore.

Malik sat up with her still in his lap and hugged her tightly from behind.

"Are you enjoying yourself?" he asked as he wiped her hair out of her face, tugging at her long hair, gripping it into a ponytail.

"Yes," she whispered.

He lay back down on the bed, holding her, giving her a small break—time to recuperate from the orgasms. He turned sideways, spooning her, gripped her breasts and kissed her neck once again.

"You're so wet," he said, grunting as he pumped his body slowly, trying to hold back on his orgasm. He pushed into her a few more times, then he was yelling out in pure pleasure. When he thought he'd finished, his penis pulsated more and more. He squeezed Sammie tight, gasping as his body jerked from his strong release, over and over.

They stay in this position as they drifted off to sleep.

CHAPTER 23

MYSTERIOUS SITUATION

WILLIAM

William pushed the closet door completely opened. He stood there in shock, looking at a red candle that was lit on the floor inside of the closet and the two books, which he'd placed outside in the garage now sat beside the candle. He walked into the closet slowly, blew out the candle, then picked up the books, almost to ensure that they were real and walked back downstairs and into the kitchen, dropping the books off there. He did one more sweep around the first floor of his house, then he opened his front door and circled the premises, looking to see if Casey is anywhere in sight. That was the only explanation. Casey must have gotten into his house somehow.

As William circled back to the front for a third time, as he was about to enter his door, he saw the herbs that were in the package in the garage sprinkled at the ledge of his door. Taking his foot, he kicked the snake root away in anger and frustration.

"What is going on?" he asked out loud to himself.

"Who are you talking to?" Sara asked as she walked up to him in the doorway. "And, why are you sweating? William, are you okay?" she asked, putting the back of her hand to his head.

"When did you get here?" William asked.

"I just pulled up. You didn't hear my car?" she questioned,

perplexed. "Are you feeling okay?" Sara put the bag of Chinese food down on the porch and looked down at the snake root herb that was sprinkled across the porch before picking up a few of the pieces. "What's this? William. Were you smoking?"

William didn't respond to Sara's inquiry. He grabbed the bag of Chinese food and walked toward her. "Come on. Let's go inside," he said as he ushered her in, then peeked out once more before closing the front door and locking it.

Sara grabbed the bag of food from William and walked into the kitchen, placed it on the island in the center of the room. William walked up to the counter and stood there in a daze as Sara continued to unload the bag, she watched William carefully, and before walking over to the cabinet to grab plates out, she asked, "Have you been drinking?"

He shook his head.

"What's wrong? You look like you saw a ghost."

His eyes met hers. "Something like that, I guess. I was working on the case in the office and…I thought I heard something. I was just checking around the house to make sure. Nothing was there."

Sara glanced at the two books on the edge of the kitchen island. "What is this?" she asked, picking up the books off the counter.

"Some things that Casey left," William said, very reserved.

Sara flipped through the pages of one of the books then said, "She was into stuff like this."

"How deep?"

"Very deep. Remember that story I told you about our trip to Montego Bay?"

"Yes."

"That's when it all started. She stayed in contact with those two guys, you know, the Haitian and Cambodian? They came up to visit her once or twice. I saw them on campus with her. She called them her long-lost brothers. Of course everybody just thought she was getting freaky with two guys, including me."

Sara slid William's plate of food over to him and they both ate, sitting at the barstools around the counter.

"My great-grandmother came from the islands. I hear stories all the time about the dark arts and occult practices." Sara paused and went into thought then said, "I don't really believe in that stuff, do you?"

William responded, "I didn't."

"Well, some people don't believe in God, but He's real in my book. Just because science can't prove or disprove the supernatural aspects of life, it doesn't mean it doesn't exist. Think about it, there is no way to measure pain, or no way to measure how someone feels. Those are all subjective based on what a person reports. People could lie about their pain level to get drugs and people could lie about their emotions to hide their feelings."

"Where are you going with this, Sara?" William asked irritably.

"Just like we believe in a higher source, others could believe in and worship lower entities or idols. The Bible talks about that."

"So, you think voodoo and other deities that people worship really exist?"

"Yes. I think dark entities are the essence of those who turn away from God and feed negativity into the world."

"I never knew you felt that way."

"Well, like I said, everyone doesn't discuss their true feelings about things so openly."

"So, what do you think would happen as a result of someone worshipping deities?"

"I don't want to talk about it. It gives me chills just thinking of my trip to Jamaica with Casey."

William took a deep breath. Thinking he needed to reread that report on the Obeah practices that Lamar wrote up for him. This time he would read it from a newfound perspective. As of late, all of these new experiences were throwing him off guard. His memories took him back to Casey sitting in his closet chanting around that same red candle that was in the middle of the floor tonight. Also, the video that Samantha captured of Casey at the police station, a little while back, which seemed satanic, like something was invading her body, trying to escape. Now this.

William and Casey finished up in the kitchen. She walked with him to his office. When he got back to the computer, it was dark. "Hmm, I guess my laptop died," he said, pushing the power button, then searching his briefcase for the power cord. He plugged it in and let it charge.

"What were you researching?" Sara asked.

"It's a video from Club Enticement—the night that Malik was poisoned."

"I see," Sara said, nodding. "Well, was it her?"

"I don't know. I was just about to find out when I got distracted by the noise, then you came," he said, turning to look at Sara.

She looked at him bright eyed. "Okay. I could get my laptop out of the car while yours charge."

William hesitated before saying, "That's okay. I'll wait a little while. I think I need to lay down for a little bit anyways. Do you wanna watch Netflix?" he asked.

"Or we could do something else, to help ease your mind," she said.

William smiled, but wasn't feeling in the mood. His mind was wandering in so many directions, but the thought he couldn't get off his mind was how Sara conveniently showed up right as all of these mysterious things started happening.

CHAPTER 24

KELVIN'S FRUSTRATION

Kelvin jumped out of his truck and walked into his office. The two loads he'd picked up and dropped off today had left him feeling exhausted, especially with them being hours away. He'd been sort of moody all day trying to figure out what was going on with Sabine. He was normally able to read her so clearly. She seemed temperamental and flustered with him last night.

He took his work gloves off and threw them on his desk, which had papers scattered all over. He sat at his desk chair and twirled around as his mind took him back to the dinner last night at the house.

She invited William over, he thought, *but why didn't she let me know beforehand he was joining us for dinner? I don't trust William. He still has the hots for Sabine. I can see it in the way he looks at her and the way he seems to always have his cruddy hands all over her. And why does he always slip away with her when she excuses herself from the room? Whenever I'm occupied with something, he slides right over to her and is all in her face. Like at the grand opening last week...his arm was wrapped around her waist and Sabine returned the gesture. Maybe she wants him. And who the hell is Amanda? She met her at Club Enticement one time and now they're all buddy-buddy? Why does she think I'm wrong for caring about what happened to her on the road that night when she called the tow truck? I can't be a concerned fiancé?*

Kelvin's cell phone rang and he answered without looking at

the caller ID, putting his wireless headset on. "What's up? This is Kelvin," he stated.

"Hi, handsome," said the seductive feminine voice across the other end of the phone.

He looked at the caller ID and didn't recognize the phone number."

Who is this?" he asks.

"You don't remember me? Well, it's been a few months now. Darleen... in Jacksonville." She paused. "You met me at Waves Logistics—the dispatcher. You said when you opened your office in Jacksonville you would hire me?"

"Oh, yes. Hi Darleen."

"I've been told you've been back several times. Why haven't you come in to see me?"

"Just busy, trying to get in and get out quickly," he said.

"Well, you know this is the one-stop shop. You could have picked up your load and a little sumtin' sumtin' too, if you know what I mean?" she asked and laughed.

Kelvin smiled, partly entertained but mostly feeling desired. "I'll be there tomorrow around noon," he said.

"Okay. Save this number in your phone. I'll be waiting on your call."

"Alright," Kelvin said with a slight smile.

"See you tomorrow," Darleen hung up the phone.

Kelvin saved her number as Jacksonville Dispatcher. Smiling to himself, he collapsed his head into his hands, took a deep breath in and then blew it out slowly. "What am I doing?" he asked. He picked up his phone and dialed his brother.

"What up, Kelv?" his brother yelled across the phone.

"Hey, Milton."

"What up? You good?" Milton asked.

"I don't know. Things are so busy lately I haven't really had a chance to think about how everything's unfolding."

"You havin' second thoughts about marriage?"

"Ummm."

"Who is she?"

"Who is who?" Kelvin asked.

"I know you, brother. Dad told me about Sabine, but why haven't you invited me down to Florida? You've got me running this business up in Michigan like I own it."

"Well, I'm coming up next month to sign papers to make you co-owner. I really appreciate all of your help."

"I know, and all of the loot we makin'," Milton said, chuckling.

"Yeah."

"So, who is she?" Milton asked.

"What are you talking about man?" Kelvin asked, annoyed.

"Who's the other woman?"

"What made you say that?"

"I hear it in your voice. You sound conflicted. Plus, I knew it was only a matter of time for you."

Kelvin took in what his brother had just said, thinking back to over the years about his problem with committing in relationships, after things went south with Jaysha, the love of his life at one time.

"I haven't cheated on Sabine. It's different with her," Kelvin said, thinking back on their mini vacation to Key West and his "almost unfaithfulness" with Cindy. He contemplated to himself, *Old habits die hard.*

"Uh-huh."

"It's just...I don't know how to do this. This is new territory for me. I'm use to bolting when things get tough."

"Well, don't go do nothing stupid. From what dad tells me, Sabine's a beauty and a keeper."

Kelvin smiled. "Thank you, Milton, for picking up. I appreciate you, man."

"It's all good. Seriously, when are you gonna invite me down?"

"Soon. Let me talk it over with Sabine first."

"Alright. Handle that. Don't leave me hanging too long," Milton said before hanging up the phone.

The phone rang. It was Sabine. He answered, "Hi, sweetie."

"Hi. I made dinner. I'm waiting on you with nothing but a smile on," she said.

S.L. HARRIS

"Awwwww, sweetie. I *am* hungry. I'll be there in fifteen minutes," Kelvin said, ecstatic.

"Okay. Drive safe. Don't get a ticket," she said then hung up the phone.

Wow! Kelvin thinks to himself, *I actually made it home in fifteen minutes. That's a record. If I had truly been going the speed limit, it would have taken me about twenty-five minutes.* He rushed out of the car, unlocked the front door, took his shoes off, and walked in through the kitchen. No Sabine. The lights were dimmed in the house. He walked to the bedroom. Still no sign of Sabine. Then from the bedroom window, he saw candles lit outside. They were laid out strategically on a pink blanket, all white, in the shape of a heart. On the center of the blanket was Sabine with a see-through robe on. Kelvin walked outside the sliding patio door that connected from the room and the dining room.

"Hi, Kelvin," Sabine said softly reaching toward him.

He walked toward her as she stood to greet him. Kelvin bent and kissed her lips softly.

"Sit," she said as she forced him to sit with his legs folded across and under, sitting Indian style on the blanket. She then placed a blindfold over his eyes and kissed him again tenderly then very passionately. She stopped abruptly.

"Why did you stop?" Kelvin asked.

"You said you were hungry, right?" she asked.

"Yes, but I want you more," he replied.

"You will have me, but I have to feed my man if I want to keep him, right? We're going to play a game. If you can guess the first three foods I place in your mouth, you'll be rewarded."

She placed something against his lips. It felt cool and wet to Kelvin.

"Open your mouth. Good. Now bite down," she said.

Kelvin chewed on the mysterious food she'd just placed in his mouth. "Glazed strawberries with whipped cream," he said between bites.

96

"Yes. Good job, Kelvin, but that was an easy one. It gets harder as the game goes on."

"Oh, I know baby," he said rubbing his hand lightly across his penis.

She giggled.

Next, Kelvin smelled something fried. Sabine placed it in his mouth. He chewed. It was crunchy, seasoned very well, slight taste of fish. "Fried calamari," he mumbled as pieces of the food fell from his lips.

"Really good, Kelvin," she said as she smooched his lips, nibbling on some of the crumbs.

He wrapped his arms around her, and they fell stretched out onto the blanket. His hands were over her booty squeezing her cheeks and pulling her into him with force.

"Wait, wait, Kelvin. You have one more," she said as she pulled at his hand to have him sit up again.

"Oh, actually, you can lay down for this." She pushed him gently down to the blanket. "This could make you hot after you try it, so let's take some of your clothes off," she said as she pulled his jeans down. She put something up to his face. It smelled fried and with a lot of spice. Kelvin took a bite. As he chewed on it, Sabine poured something warm all over his penis then said, "Keep your eyes closed and the blindfold on." The next thing Kelvin felt was her mouth on his testicles licking softly, then gentle sucks slowly emerged.

"What does the food taste like?" she asked him.

As he chewed, it reminded him of patting his head and rubbing his stomach at the same time. He had two separate things going on at once; her sweet lips on him, in the most delicate area of his body, licking and sucking, while he chewed on the tastiest piece of chicken he's ever had. But the more he chewed and the more she sucked, he forgot how to swallow. Finally, he gulped the piece of food down. Sabine moved up to his penis and traced her tongue up and down the shaft.

"Ummm," was all Kelvin could muster out.

"Kelvin, you taste delicious," she said then placed her lips around the head of his penis, using her tongue to circle the tip, then her mouth became like a vacuum. She was up and down, up and down several times, keeping her motions steady.

Kelvin began to sway his hips upward.

She stopped. "So, what was the last thing you ate?" she asked.

"I don't know. Some type of meat with spices. Chicken?" He asked.

She crawled on top of him and whispered, "Wrong. Chicken fried steak with hot sauce. I'll give you a bonus chance in order to continue tonight's escapades." She kissed him. Her lips interlaced with his, her tongue touched the tip of his before she pulled away. "What did you just taste on my lips?" she asked.

"Is this a trick question?" Kelvin asked, smiling.

"No," she said as she backed away, moving off his body.

"Your mouth tasted sweet...chocolate syrup," Kelvin blurted out, taking the blindfold off and reaching for her, pulling her down on top of him. "Was I right on the bonus question?"

"Yes," she said with a smirk. Kelvin pulled away from Sabine a little, enough so that he could put one of her nipples in his mouth. She was all moans.

As Kelvin made his early-morning commute to Jacksonville, he rubbed the back of his neck and shoulders, thinking he could use an extra two hours of sleep at least. Riding exhausted on a dark road at four a.m. was not safe, especially in his condition. Everything that his truck driving classes taught him about road safety was on the line. He was violating at least three codes. After the night he and Sabine had, he should have taken a personal day.

His thoughts took him back to those sweet, sacred moments he'd spent with her. The wine, the glazed dipped strawberries, the whipped cream, the out-of-this-world sex. *The feeling she gives me, shit!* Kelvin thought as his whole body jerked, sensing the pleasure down in his pelvic area. Seeing as to how the night ended at one o'clock in the morning, it was no wonder he couldn't keep his eyes opened. And his focus...well, that was way off base. His mind kept wandering back to how satisfying her lips felt around him—in more ways than one. Like a movie replaying in his mind's eye, he saw her soft brown skin in the moonlight outside. He could feel her body rubbing against his skin, warm and moist, sliding together conjoined. They were a perfect fit.

He exited the dark freeway, found a parking space at a rest stop, walked to the back of his truck, and took out his phone where he had recorded videos of him and Sabine during the act last night. As he lay down on the bed, his hand gravitated toward his semi-erect penis.

CHAPTER 25

WILLIAM'S REMORSE/ PARANOIA

William lay in bed with Sara at his side, looking down at her questionably. She was hugged up close to him. She came back into his life so easily after his unfaithfulness to her, and not just with a random woman, but with Casey Ingram, Sara's college roommate. William's remorse of his own actions, in the recent past, was making him question Sara's very reasons for being there tonight.

William thought, *Isn't it ironic I feel suspicious of Sara when it was me who cheated on her with her friend, Casey. It was me who asked Casey out on a date? It was me who took her out to dinner and invited her back to my house afterward. It was me who offered her a drink from the mini bar upstairs, knowing where things were headed. Yeah, but it was Casey who straddled her legs around me as we sat on the sofa drinking and talking. It was her who said, "You have something on your face," as she held her drink and sat on my lap pretending to search for something, grinding her body onto mine, making me lose all sense of any rational reality that I had, forgetting I was in a happy and sexually satisfying relationship with Sara at the time. But it was me who took her drink from her hand, set it on the end table and said, "There's nothing on my face. If you want to kiss me, I won't stop you."*

It was Sara who walked upstairs after coming in from working late, who saw us naked on the sofa in the loft, who woke me up by softly calling my name several times, as she sat across from us on the coffee table looking at the mess I had gotten myself into. When I tried to explain my position, she shushed me and said, "No words can undo this." Sara threw her key down on the table and left.

William continues to think to himself, *So, why is Sara forgiving of me and why now? It all seemed too coincidental that she showed up tonight just as all of these bazaar things were taking place around my house. I knew she didn't have a key, plus I had the locks changed on all of my doors after the incident where Casey went ape shit after I asked her to leave my home. Casey was arrested when the cops saw her put her hands on me out of anger of my request, then she resisted arrest, shit, that's how this whole mess started!*

How could Casey have gotten into my garage tonight? Could Ms. Santos, my cleaning lady, have left the garage door open at some point? Maybe taking the trash out? Could Sara and Casey be working together? But at what avail? What would Sara want from me at this time?

Sara shifted around, moving in closer to William. She groaned tenderly, then slowly moved her hand to touch William's private area. He pulled her curly black hair from her face to see that her eyes were still closed.

Then she said, "You're so good. It's like we never skipped a beat." She climbed over William, and when she is face to face with him, kissed his lips and slid up and out of the bed. "I need to go home and shower, get ready for the day," she said.

"Okay," William responded.

"Let me know if you need my help with the case." She grabbed her clothes off the floor and her bag off the chair and exited the room.

William heard the front door closed behind her. He walked out of his room, opened the door, and watched as Sara got into her car.

As William sat at his computer, he realized he was still perplexed by last night's events. But then again, maybe Sara just missed him, she seemed sincere these past few days. As he opened his laptop, he press control-alt-delete and entered his password. The video popped back up paused right in the position it was before the computer went blank last night. He pressed the play button. He could see a top angled view of a woman walking down the hall, but it was fuzzy and the fact that it was in black and white, it was hard to make out the figure.

Think, William, he says to himself. *What was Casey wearing that night we went out? She was gone for a good little while when we were at Club Enticement, long enough for me to watch Sabine seduce Kelvin in that small private room. Oh, Sabine was so beautiful on her knees, pleasing him. I wish it was me sitting in that chair and not Kelvin... Focus, William. What was Casey wearing that night at the club?*

"I have pictures in my phone," he said out loud to himself. He grabbed his Android and commenced to press on the gallery button. As he was scrolling through, he saw they'd taken a couple of pictures at a bar before the club. Casey had on a short tight body dress with black sequins all over it. Her hair was slicked up on top of her head with a long weave ponytail falling down the length of her back.

He clicked back to the video, rewound it, and watched closely as the woman walked toward the camera. The angle made it difficult to see the body completely, but what caught his eye was when she passed the camera, she grinned, and when she lifted her head up as if laughing, he identifies her smile, perfectly white teeth, and high cheekbones.

"There it is," he said, staring at the frozen screen with the lower portion of Casey's face in view. He hurriedly looked through his phone to find a close-up shot of her face with a similar angle. Once he'd found the picture. He used his camera phone to take a picture of the computer screen with her face frozen there, then emailed both pictures to Detective Mack, then began preparing paperwork to submit both photos into evidence.

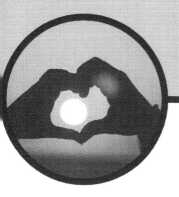

CHAPTER 26

THE WORK DAY

KELVIN

Kelvin made it to Jacksonville by 9:45 a.m., after dropping off a load and securing another one to the truck. He walked inside of the dispatch office of Waves Logistics. As he was walking over to an empty desk, he was greeted by a very excited voice from behind. "Kelvin! You made it!"

Kelvin turned. "Yes, I did." He looked at a woman who had a name tag that read *Darleen Smiley*. "Ms. Smiley, nice to see you again, "Kelvin said, trying to connect her face to the first time he'd met her but immediately recognizing her voice from the phone conversation the day before.

She reached out to hug him. "It's so good to see you again," she stated, pulling away from the hug and touching his chest as she looked him up and down.

"Nice to see you too," he smiled, taking in her features.

She stood about five feet four inches tall, had brown skin, and an hour glassed shape and weighed about one hundred and sixty pounds. She wore a grey sweater over a white cami shirt. *She has a pretty face,* Kelvin thought, *and looks to be in her late thirties or early forties.*

"If you have a little time. I go on my lunch break in a few minutes."

"I have time," Kelvin said.

"Okay. Have a seat. Make yourself comfortable. I'll be right back." She hurried off.

Kelvin took a deep breath and sat in the chair facing her desk awaiting her return.

She came back into the room with newly applied red lipstick and without her sweater. "Okay, I'm ready. There's a place right up the street we could eat at," she says waiting on Kelvin to stand.

As Kelvin stood, she grabbed his hand and led him out of the back garage. They jumped into her Honda Civic and arrived at their location, a little diner in town, two minutes later. After being seated at a table, she asked, "So, what's new?" then grinned widely.

Kelvin's gaze darted to her cleavage, which was very hard to miss, seeing as she had on a very low-cut cami shirt. Maybe it wasn't that the cami was low cut, but more so that her breast were huge!

"Ummm, nothing much," he replied, sipping the water their waitress left for them.

"I haven't heard from you in a few months."

"Yeah. Just busy with the business. I've been working a lot of hours these days, traveling in and out of state."

"I can imagine. So business is good?"

"Very," Kelvin said and smiled at her, looking directly into her eyes now remembering their first encounter a few months back, before Sabine, at the new orientation party at Waves. The owner thought it would be good for Kelvin to mingle as sister companies associated with Waves Logistics were in attendance. That's when he saw Darleen. She was dancing on the floor with a beer in her hand. She had on a mini skirt and low-cut top. Kelvin pushed up to her with his beer in hand, and they danced the night away.

"You told me the last time we met you were living out of a hotel. Have you found something permanent now?"

"Yes. Something is currently in the works."

"Okay. Okay," she said, nodding. "Look at you getting all settled. Well, you know if you workin' a late night in Jacksonville, you could always crash at my place instead of sleeping in your truck, or at a cheap hotel, or risk driving back to Tampa."

"Thank you. I appreciate that offer…" Kelvin was cut short by the waitress returning to the table to take their orders.

Afterward, Kelvin got a text from Sabine. *Hi, babe. Thank you for the sexcapades last night. I hope you're getting some rest in between loads. I'm exhausted today. Anyways, I wanted to let you know I invited William over for dinner. He has something he wants to go over concerning the case with Casey. Are you okay with this?*

Kelvin looked away from his phone and rolled his eyes, choosing not to respond to the text due to his irritation with this situation with William. He put his phone back in his pocket.

"Everything good?" Darleen asked.

"Yeah… I'm good," he said as he wondered about William and Sabine's relationship. He tried to control the rage that was erupting in his chest by taking a few deep breaths. "Darleen, can you excuse me, please? I need to make a call." Kelvin walked out of the restaurant and called Sabine.

He dialed and waited on her to pick up, but the call was sent to voicemail. He called the business phone of S & S Café and Lounge. Lamar picked up.

"Thank you for calling S& S Café. Lamar speaking. How can I help you?"

"Good morning, Lamar. This is Kelvin, Sabine's fiancé."

"Hi, Kelvin. How are you?"

"Great," Kelvin said monotone, "Is Sabine around?"

"She just went upstairs with a client. Do you need me to get her?"

"No, it's okay. I'll try her later," Kelvin said then hung up. He stood outside for a few minutes calming himself down before going back into the diner.

Darleen was eating when he returned to the table. Kelvin sat and picked up his fork to cut into his omelet. He looked up at her then asked, "So, do you stay around here?"

"Yes. I'm about ten minutes away. I have a nineteen-year-old who lives with me, but he's over his girlfriend's place most of the time."

"Listen, I have a few runs in Jacksonville today. Maybe after I can stop by for a visit," Kelvin said with his eyebrow raised.

"Okay. That's fine by me," she said giddy, "I'm cooking oxtails. You eat that kinda food?"

"Oh yeah, baby," Kelvin replied with a slight grin.

CHAPTER 27

THE SESSION WITH AMANDA

SABINE

It was a little after five p.m., and Sabine was headed over to Amanda's. Just as she pulled into the driveway, she looked down at her phone at a text message that had just come through from Kelvin.

> *Sabine,*
>
> *I am out of town for a few days in Jacksonville as I told you yesterday. Am I okay with another man coming to my house for dinner while I'm away? No! But I know you're a grown woman and will make up your own mind on what you feel is right.*

Sabine called Kelvin immediately. No answer. She threw her phone into her purse, angered by Kelvin's response, then pulled the phone back out and texted:

> *Kelvin*
>
> *If you aren't okay with it, then I won't invite him over. I'll call to cancel. It's that simple. Why do you feel the*

*need to play mind games with me lately? Is it that you
don't trust me because you're doing your dirt? You are
gone an awful lot these days. Are you living a second life
in Jacksonville?*

Sabine exited the car leaving her purse and cell phone on
the front seat, only taking her keys. She rang the doorbell to
Amanda's home and waited impatiently, thinking about Kelvin
and his smart-ass text message.

Amanda opened the door.

"Hi, sweetie. Come in," she said after hugging Sabine briefly
and stepping back for her to walk in. As Sabine had a seat at
her kitchen table, which seems to be their meeting spot lately,
Amanda studied her for a while. "I'll make us some chamomile
tea. You can just start with what's bugging you right now," she
said as she walked over to the stove.

"What I don't understand about Kelvin is why he feels so
insecure when it comes to me and my relationship with William?"
Sabine blurted out. "I mean, I've never given him a reason to
doubt my faithfulness to him… Kelvin, on the other hand, has
shaken my trust, and I struggle with it every day, but you don't
see me questioning his every move."

Amanda sat down across from Sabine and cupped both her
hands into hers then closed her eyes, taking several deep breaths.
Sabine joined her in the deep-breathing exercise, which helped to
calm Sabine's nerves and open her heart to receive the message
Amanda was ready to give her.

"Now, who is William, sweetheart?" she asked with her eyes
still closed.

"A friend of mine. He used to be a client before we were
friends."

"Okay. Take a deep breath," she said.

"I see him now. He was the guy at the table that night at the
club, with the woman I warned you about."

"Yes," Sabine responded calmly.

"I see." Amanda opened her eyes as the teakettle went off.

As she was walking over to pour the tea, she spoke. "Kelvin has a right to be suspicious of your relationship with William."

Sabine looked up toward her as she was walking back to the table to bring the cups of tea.

"William is in love with you. Kelvin senses it."

"I know but, that gives him no right—"

"Honey, honey, it doesn't excuse Kelvin's behavior lately. And, you've done nothing wrong."

Sabine sipped her tea.

"Remember we discussed twin flames and you two being a mirror for each other to help work through the ego mind?"

"Yes."

"This is what's occurring. This is the middle part, where all the magic and healing begins. This is the unscripted part of the fairy tale. Kelvin loves you, but he has his own issues to work through, just as you do. We talked about twin flames, but not about soulmates. A soulmate is someone who offers you support and makes life a little easier. They could be a family member, friend, or lover."

"Okay," Sabine replied, nodding, wondering where Amanda was going with this.

"They offer solace when life gets hard, whereas a twin flame forces you to deal with the parts of yourself you aren't willing to look at. Can you see the difference?"

"Yes."

"William is your soulmate. You both offer each other support and comfort in the time of need. Let that sink in, sweetheart."

"But what does that mean?"

"It means you met two men who are both in love with you. It doesn't mean you stop being friends with William, as he will be whatever it is you want him to be to you this lifetime. It means there is a lesson in this for you, Kelvin, and William." Amanda paused for a while, then continued, "So, how is the technique working for you? Are you able to successfully block Kelvin out of your head?"

"Oh my God, yes," Sabine exclaimed.

Amanda laughed. "With you and Kelvin, it's about setting boundaries with each other—drawing a line on how much you are willing to let him experience through you and vice versa, and how much he is willing to do to maintain the relationship. You see, he's good at starting things, but not so good at maintaining them. He's the runner in your relationship. Except this time, he doesn't really want to run—it's just a pattern he's used to."

Sabine drank most of her tea down as she sat quietly taking in what Amanda had shared with her.

Amanda looked at Sabine then said, "You are going to be okay. You are going to get through this just fine. Just stand your ground and set boundaries."

Sabine checked her text messages before pulling off to drive home. Kelvin didn't text her back. She arrived home to find William's car sitting in front of the house. As she pulled into the driveway, William exited his car and walked over to hers. Sabine rolled her window down, "I'm sorry. Were you waiting long?" she asked.

"No worries, love, only a few minutes."

He opened her car door and walked with her toward the house.

"I haven't started dinner," Sabine said, turning to face him as she put her key in the lock.

"I could pick something up for us," he said as they walked into the house.

"No, I can whip something up. I just hope you aren't starving," she replied as she walked toward the kitchen to wash her hands.

"I'm good. It gives me some time to explain what's been going on while you cook. I could assist in the kitchen, if you'd like."

"Sure," Sabine said, stepping away from the sink so he could wash his hands. She looked in the refrigerator and grab some turkey sausage, onions, and bell peppers, then she looked into the pantry and grabbed a bag of rice and two cans of black beans. "We need a pot and a skillet," Sabine said to William, pointing in the direction of pans. She grabbed the chopping board as William took the pans out of the cabinet. "Can you rinse those out for me and add three cups of water to the pot and a half cup of water to the skillet with three tablespoons of olive oil?"

"Just so you know, I have no problems taking orders from you, Sabine," William said and looked back at Sabine and smiled.

She shook her head and laughed out loud. "Okay. Noted," she said.

He walked over to her side and watched as she chopped the onions and bell peppers, then he began to speak, taking a seat at the counter where she was chopping.

"So, I left the café before coming here. I stopped in to see Sammie about the case. She's glowing."

"I know, right? Sammie and Malik are so happy now and expecting a baby. Can you believe that?"

Sabine thought about how Casey was so overly concerned about Sammie not giving Malik a child, and now ironically after everything that had transpired, Sammie was pregnant. "I'm pleased they're putting this Casey thing behind them. So, how is the case going?"

"Very good. I was able to pin Casey's face on the video around the time Sammie said she and Malik left that room."

"Yeah? What time was that?" Sabine asked as she moved over to the stove with the chopping board in hand to pour the onions, bell peppers, and sausage into the skillet.

"It was 11:11 p.m.," William stated. "But that's not what I wanted to talk about."

"I'm listening," Sabine said as she pour the rice into the boiling water and put a top over the sausage after seasoning it.

"Some weird things are happening in my house lately."

Sabine thought about making a joke about his and Sara's wild and crazy sex life, tying it into the "weird things" happening in his house, but she remembered how he got a little offended a few days ago and decided against it. She looked in his eyes, and she could sense he needed her undivided attention, so she turned the rice down and placed a top over it, then asked, "Do you want to have some wine while the food gets ready and sit out on the patio and talk?"

"Yes. That would be great," William said.

"Okay. I don't have any of that expensive wine we had the other day, but pick something out of the refrigerator or pantry. I'm going to use the bathroom, be right back," Sabine said as she walked into the room. She put her purse away in the closet and took out her cell phone to charge it. Before doing that, she sent Kelvin a text message.

CHAPTER 28

KELVIN'S UNEXPECTED GUEST

Kelvin finished his last load around eight p.m. He parked his truck across the street from the La Quinta Inns & Suites and walked over and checked into a room. He took a long, hot shower while thinking about Sabine's text message.

Living a second life? What the hell? I'm trying to build a new life with her!

Before Kelvin's thoughts could anger him anymore, his phone rang. He reached for his phone, which was sitting on the top of the toilet outside the shower and answered, "This is Kelvin."

"And this is Darleen. Listen, change of plans. My son is home tonight. Seems as if he and his girlfriend got into some type of argument. I packed up the food, and I'm en route to your hotel. Do you still stay at the La Quinta Inn?"

"Ummm, yes," Kelvin said, having second thoughts about this whole situation.

"Okay. I'll be there in two minutes," Darleen said excitedly and hung up the phone.

"Fuck!" Kelvin yelled. He turned the water off and grabbed his towel, sliding on the mat he put down in front of the shower and falling onto his butt. "Ouch," he bellowed.

He heard a knock on the door a minute later.

This is too much, he thought. He wrapped the towel around his waist and walk toward the door. When he opened it, Darleen walked right in with a crockpot in her hands and a bag on her shoulder.

Kelvin turned to look at her after looking outside the door as if to see if anyone saw her walk in, then closed and locked the door. He rubbed his hand over his moist face, exasperated by this whole situation. But, who could he be mad at? Kelvin thought. *I put myself here. Exactly the type of scenario Sabine was ranting about in her text. Shit.*

After Darleen placed the crockpot on the dresser, she turned to look at Kelvin who was her personification of the perfect man. He was six foot four inches, slender with a nice muscular built. His skin was smooth and soft looking. He looked even more tantalizing the way the moisture glistened in the light. His hair was curly and thick, and that brooding facial expression had Darleen ready to push him down to the bed and rip that towel right off him.

"Wow," she said, eyeing him up and down.

"I'm sorry." He looked down at the towel wrapped around his waist. "I was in the shower when you called me. I didn't have time to get dressed. I was going—"

Darleen cut him off. "Please don't apologize. This is...perfectly okay with me."

She giggled, then turned around and pulled a bottle of wine and two cups out of the bag, then two bowls and spoons. She opened the pot and scooped two helpings of oxtail stew into each of the bowls, then handed him one. She opened the wine and poured some in both cups.

Kelvin got a whiff of the stew. It smelled so good, and he hadn't eaten since their brunch earlier that afternoon. He sat on the bed and spooned some into his mouth, one spoonful after another. "Darleen, these oxtails are delicious."

"I'm happy you're enjoying it. I have plenty, so eat up," she said as she watched him sit with his legs spread apart, hoping he'd open his legs a little wider so the towel would slide open and give her a pleasant surprise.

As she sipped her wine, she looked in the general area of his penis and noticed the imprint. Kelvin was totally oblivious to her lustful stare. He walked over to the pot, "Is it okay if I get more?" he asked, motioning to the oxtail stew.

"Help yourself. I made it for you," she said as she walked over closer to him, her double D's brushing up against his back. When he turned around, she took the bowl from him, set it on the dresser and moved in closer to him. Her body against his. She rubbed his stomach, then walked her fingers up to his chest, circling his nipples.

Kelvin breathed in, trying to ignore the fact that he was becoming erect. He looked upward toward the ceiling, trying to think of anything but this woman's hands on his body, but it wasn't working. His thoughts were taking him to how turned on he'd been since this morning after Sabine and his sexual escapade last night, and how frustrated he was about their little spat via text, and how it would feel really good to take out some of that repressed anger. He lowered his face to Darleen, reaching out to grab her breast, but decided against that and put his hands down by his side and lifted up his chin and took a deep breath.

Darleen grabbed his hands and stepped back, walking closer to the bed. He stepped toward her. She took down the spaghetti straps to her sundress and scooted out of it, letting it fall to the floor, then placed both his hands onto her bare breasts as she fell to the bed with him on top of her. Nothing separated them but the towel, which was still wrapped around his waist. He squeezed her breast softly, hesitantly, at first, then as passion took over his mind and body, he gripped them tightly, gliding his tongue across each of her nipples, and smashing his body on hers, gyrating his hips, imagining how it would feel inside of her. Kelvin lifted up to take the towel from his waist, but just before he did he heard his phone go off in the bathroom.

"I'm sorry, Darleen. I have to get that," he said as he lifted completely off the bed and walked into the bathroom. He opened his texts and found a message from Sabine:

Sweetie,

I'm sorry. I was way out of line with the text message I sent to you earlier. I've just been missing you a lot lately. I feel it isn't my place to tell you to stop being on the road so much. I knew this about you from our first date. It's just that I feel lonely. I feel like you're pulling away from me, and I need you right now…here with me. Come back to me.

I love you,

Sabine

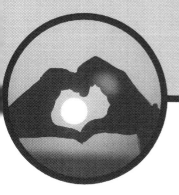

CHAPTER 29

DINNER WITH WILLIAM

Sabine walked back into the kitchen and added the beans to the rice then turned the pot off. She stirred the sausage and peppers and turned that pot off also.

"William!" she shouted toward the patio.

"Yes?" He peeked into the house holding his wineglass.

"Can you set the table outside?"

"Sure."

"The plates are in the cabinet over there." Sabine pointed to the right. "I'm going to take a quick shower."

Sabine joined William after her shower, wearing sweat pants and Kelvin's white t-shirt. The table was set so elegantly.

"This looks nice," Sabine said to William as she took a seat adjacent to him.

"I make it do what it do," he said and laughed vociferously.

Sabine just smiled at him.

"Dig in," he said.

"So, what did you want to talk to me about?" she asked in between bites of food.

William proceeded to tell her of all of the unusual things that had happened in his house over the past few days—from the lit candle in his closet to the snake root herbs at his door step. He even told her of his suspicion of Sara, seeing as to how she and Casey were roommates in college at one time and she seemed to show up the same night all of these supernatural occurrences were taking place.

"I have someone I want you to meet," Sabine said to him. "Well, you've met her already, at the club. Her name is Amanda."

"Oh yeah? The woman who tried to hit on you that night?"

"I don't know about that, but she's becoming a good friend of mine now. I think she could help you with some of this…"

"Well, anything that could help me sort through this, I'm open to," Williams said, chewing his food.

"I'll call her tomorrow, see if we can arrange something for us all to meet. She's teaching me a lot."

"So, how are you and Kelvin?" William asked, looking up from his plate.

"It's a sore subject right now. I'd rather not discuss it."

"I understand. Just remember when and if you ever need to talk, I'm always here. It doesn't matter the time of day or night. I'm just a phone call or text message away."

Sabine smiled, thinking on what Amanda said in regards to William being her soulmate. It was very comfortable with him. This dinner tonight, his help with the meal and setting the table, and his availability to spend time with her casually, it just warmed Sabine's heart. "Thank you, William. You're a wonderful friend."

"Anytime, Sabine. Thank you for inviting me to dinner tonight. I always feel better after talking with you. You add that calm that I need in my life." William stared at Sabine for several seconds then shook his head as if snapping himself out of something. "Well, let me help you clean up," he said as he took Sabine's plate and his into the kitchen.

"You don't have to, William. I can do that."

He walked back over to Sabine. "I want to." He stood only a few inches away from her face, his hazel eyes to her dark brown and they looked at each other eye to eye as they are exactly the same height without shoes. He lowered himself slightly to reach around her for the wineglasses, and Sabine snapped out of the trance that she was temporarily in.

She walked into the kitchen, behind William, bringing in the remaining trash from the table out on the patio. William turned to face her. "Will you walk me out, love?"

"Sure." She smiled as they walked toward the door. "Call me if anything weird happens at your house tonight. Kelvin's out of town, so…it should be okay for us to talk on the phone tonight."

He turned to look at her once they'd reached the front door and he put his shoes on, which he had taken off before walking all the way into her home when he first arrived. "I will." He tilted his head, moved in very close to Sabine, and planted a slow, sweet yet passionate kiss on her lips. Once. Twice. Three times before he pulled away. "I'm sorry. I shouldn't have—" he said before Sabine grabbed him close and proceeded to kiss him with passion and thirst before coming to her senses and pushing him away.

"It's okay. Now we're even. Good night, William," Sabine said, staring at him.

"I'm not sure if I want to go now," he said, walking toward her, standing even closer.

"It's best you do. Please. Call me if you need me," she said to him.

"Okay." He scratched his head and turned to open the door. Sabine watched as he started his car and drove off. As soon as Sabine was back in the house, she rested her back to the door and exhaled deeply, thinking, *That could have been bad—so bad.* All of a sudden, a pain hit her in the middle of her gut. She then saw snippets of Kelvin in her mind's eye. He looked to be pleading to her. He was sad.

She immediately ran to the bedroom and grabbed her phone to call him. He answered on the first ring.

"Hi baby," he said melancholy.

"Hi, sweetie. Are you okay?" Sabine asked.

"Yes. Why do you ask?"

"The text I sent today, it was harsh, accusatory, and all over the place. I'm so sorry. It's just I'm so scattered, and with you not being here…it's hard, Kelvin."

"I know, sweetie. I got your second text. And I'm sorry too, for being gone so much all the time. I'm going to try to finish up everything tomorrow and come home by the evening. It'll be late. I'm packing four days' worth of work into two days, but I think it's best that I'm there with you. I need you just as much as you need me, Sabine. It hurts being away from you, and I absolutely hate arguing with you."

Sabine lay down on her pillow and rubbed Kelvin's side of the bed. She felt surges of sexual energy exuding from her and Kelvin. Sabine thought back to her and Kelvin's night last night, but then her mind focused on William's kiss and the mystery that lay there. She shook her thoughts and placed a blue and pink bubble around her before Kelvin tried to tap into them. Kelvin was silent on the other end.

"What are you doing, Kelvin?"

"I'm in the bathroom, thinking about you and how I wish that I was there with you right now. Thinking on what I would do to you, how I would caress your body…" He seemed to whisper the words.

Oh, how Sabine loved the sound of his voice, especially when it was calm and low. It was like his lips were right against her ear.

CHAPTER 30

MEETING AT THE CAFE

SABINE

Amanda agreed to meet Sabine and William at the café at 10:30 a.m. Last night, Sabine filled Amanda in on the situation between Casey and William. They all had a seat near the window at the front. The food was personally prepared by Sabine for this occasion; turkey bacon, pancakes, scrambled eggs with onions and bell peppers, and mimosas. After everyone was seated, and Lamar had ensured that they all had everything needed to start brunch, Sabine said grace.

"Thank you, God, for allowing this opportunity to meet today to eat and fellowship. I ask that you bless this food so that it nourishes our bodies. I thank you for sending both Amanda and William into my life, and pray for continued love and strength in all of our relationships. In Jesus' name, Amen."

Both Amanda and William said, "Amen."

Amanda picked up her fork and butter knife, all the while looking at William as he sipped his mimosa and readied himself to eat. Then she said, "William, you and Casey dated for a little while."

William looked up. "Yes. She stayed with me a couple of months, and we dated."

"I've seen you two at Club Enticement a few times," Amanda said.

William grinned slightly then said, "We frequented the club quite a bit."

"Did you love Casey?" Amanda asked.

William stared at her as if he was really thinking hard on whether or not he loved Casey before finally saying, "I cared for her deeply. She had parts to her personality that shook my soul. It's hard to explain."

"Try," Amanda said as she forked eggs into her mouth and looked at William.

"She showed up at a time in my life where I felt like I needed something different. I was madly in love with my ex, Sara, but there was something about Casey that offered a sense of freedom in a way that I've never known before." William paused. "I'm restricted in some ways to my profession, my lifestyle, growing up the way I did and with the parents I had. I had a path laid before me that outlined who I would become, what I would inherit... Casey has a free spirit. She allowed me to be free. I felt like I could be someone different with her, not that there was a problem with who I was. Maybe I just needed a change."

Amanda nodded. "Go on."

"In the beginning, it was beautiful. Casey was this goddess of a woman who came into my life to show me how to live, but then, it started to feel empty. That's all it was...just a good time. I started to miss my ex, and when I tried to communicate this to Casey, she found a way to block my communication. She retreated more at home—she in one bedroom and me in another—and pushed more for us to go out to the club, out of town, to some party...anywhere. She kept me busy. We stayed drunk. I don't even know how I got through work during that time. Everything was a haze."

"Do you feel that she loved you, William?" Amanda asked.

"I don't know," William said then chewed his food. "I think being with me provided a place she could live rent free and have a drinking buddy. Of course there was sex—lots and lots of sex.

Sometimes, when we were in the act..." William paused and cleared his throat.

Sabine reached over and touched Williams hand. "You okay? If it's too much for you to talk about, maybe it's not time to discuss it."

"No, Sabine," Amanda said firmly. "Let him share." She looked to William who appeared more and more like a little boy who had lost his way.

Sabine looked at William, but he didn't speak. He just continued to eat his breakfast silently as if Amanda and Sabine weren't there. Sabine felt a chill all of a sudden. She looked to Amanda with searching eyes.

"What's happening?" Sabine asked.

"She still has him in her grip. He isn't able to communicate much more past what he has said." Amanda looked at William's blank eyes as he ate his breakfast. "Casey has him under her spell."

"What?" Sabine asked, putting her fork down on her plate and looking across to William. She waved her hand across his face. He was totally unresponsive to her movements, as if he was zoned out.

"That means she's close by."

"It doesn't make sense," Sabine rambled. "William's working on the case. If he can't speak on things he's witnessed with Casey, how is he going to represent Malik in court?"

"Exactly," Amanda stated. "She must have recently reactivated her incantation. Has she been around lately?"

"No one's seen or heard from her. We have no idea where she is. Wait, William did say that she came by his office the other day. She used to work at the salon next door. When is William going to snap out of this trance?" Sabine asked, flustered. "This is a total invasion of—"

Amanda put her hand on top of Sabine's. "Listen, Sabine. I triggered this on purpose. I knew if I kept pressing him to talk about her, he would stall in the most unnatural way. He'll snap out of it and won't even remember it happening. The haze he was talking about when he was with Casey...this is it." She gestured toward William. "This is why he couldn't remember things. When she felt him pulling away, she stuck her demonic claws into him and manipulated the situation."

"Okay, well, maybe we need to go upstairs, for some privacy," Sabine said as she got up from the table and walked over to Lamar asking if he could clear the table. When Sabine walked back over, William and Amanda were standing. Amanda put her arm around William and led him as they followed Sabine upstairs to her office. Sammie was in with a client next door.

"Amanda, how do we get Casey's claws out of William?" Sabine asked, panicked.

She took a deep breath as if assessing the situation.

When Sabine looked at William, he was blinking and breathing normally, but it was like he was a blank canvas, waiting on someone to draw the picture or more like plan his next move.

"Casey is smart and conniving. I should know," Amanda said, still looking at William.

Sabine turn to look at Amanda, "How?"

Amanda started to speak to William. "I know you hear me, Casey. You've been in William's head the whole time, picking up on his work and research on your case."

Sabine sat back in awe and just watched as Amanda talked to Casey through William, curious as to how she knew Casey.

"Baby girl, I'm sorry." Amanda paused with tears rolling down her cheeks. "I'm sorry our father was who he was—dark, heartless, evil. And your mother, so weak and afraid that she gave you up so easily."

Amanda rubbed William's hand, intending her affection for Casey.

"I tried to be everything you were longing for from my mother, your step-mother, Naddi, and our stepdad. Just as much as you needed a mother, I needed a daughter... When I found my mother's letters years after she passed away talking about you, the baby Samby had with his wife, it broke my heart to hear your story. What you didn't know is that Samby was my father too."

CHAPTER 31

WILLIAM'S REIKI SESSION

Samantha gathered a few oils from her massage and reiki room to put in the burner. She mixed lavender and peppermint, then asked Sabine and Amanda to help roll William on to his side. By this time, William was in a deep sleep, unawakened by talking or movement. Amanda informed the girls; Samantha and Sabine, that the body can only maintain as a host for about fifteen to thirty minutes at a time. It takes a toll on the body and sends it into shock, which was what was happening with William right now. His coping mechanism—sleep—had kicked in.

Sammie and Sabine decided to do a healing session on William before he came to in order to avoid any post-traumatic stress type situations. Sabine knew from her training that even though consciously he was not present, subconsciously he heard every word. Sammie strategically placed Sabine's right hand on William's solar plexus charka right above his navel and her left hand on his back in the area where his heart charka would be located. She asked that her sister send love and peace energetically to those areas on William's body.

Sammie grabbed a smudge stick of sage, lit it and walked around the room with it clearing out negative energies. She said a prayer of protection.

"Girls, she's gone," Amanda said. "Like I said, it takes a lot of energy to sustain something like that. Casey must be practicing the dark Obeah rituals. Our bodies aren't meant to endure those types of things. It's unnatural, evasive, and unclean. When Casey indulges in things like this, it weakens her immune system. Just as William is tired, she will sleep for twenty-four hours or more to recover."

After a few minutes of holding William, one hand on his stomach and one on his back, Sabine slowly removed her hands. She then sat on the edge of the sofa and lifted his head onto her lap as Sammie turned him onto his back and laid her hands above his forehead, moved down to his throat, then to his chest, stomach, and pelvis. She was clearing his energy field.

"How can we prevent this from happening again?" Sabine asked Amanda.

"Sabine, it's like I showed you with the blue bubble. You had to learn how to protect yourself spiritually from people's ability to gain access to you. We're all energy, and we're all connected, all a part of the universal unconsciousness. William will have to do the same as far as protecting his psychic body and aura, especially as he works on this case."

Sabine thought back on the conversation Amanda had with Casey through William. It was so unnerving. Both Sabine and Sammie were still shook. It was so up close and personal and so haunted and powerful. After it was revealed that Casey and Amanda were half-sisters, same father but different mothers, there was a silence for a few minutes. William sat as a vessel on the sofa. His breathing became heavy, his eyes rolled to the back of his head, the lights flickered in the room, and the radio automatically turned itself on, then off. Casey spoke.

It started off harsh and abrasive, which partly had to do with Casey speaking through William's vocal cords. Plus, she was angry. Although, Sabine could feel that she was speaking out of pain, fear, and lack. Casey said, "I'm tired of you people telling me how I should feel or adding pity to your hearts for me. I'm a queen. I've found my place. I don't have to hide where I am now. I can just be who I was born to be. I can know my father here. He's my ally."

Amanda asked, "If you're not hiding, where are you now?"

Casey responded, "I'm at William's doorstep if I need to be, in his garage, at Sabine's home in the foyer kissing her goodnight, in William's room making love to Sara, in this office talking to you right now."

Sammie turned to look at Sabine when Casey said at *Sabine's home kissing her goodnight*. Sabine glanced her way but kept her focus on William's body and Casey's voice.

"Where is your physical body at this time?" Amanda demanded, angered. "You need to stop playing these silly games. It's you who will get hurt. You know the rules, and you are violating every natural law, even as they pertain to Obeah's traditions. You know it! Has Samby told you the consequences of using such power? Do you know the damage it will do to your body, let alone William's? If you ever cared about William..." Amanda paused then continued. "If you care about your life and your physical body, you will stop this now."

Casey gave a very unnerving laugh, then said, "Look at you getting all upset, Amanda. The woman who couldn't have any babies of her own. The woman who needed me to fill her motherly urge. Well, how are you feeling now about the girl you helped raised? You don't want to take credit for who I've become? Why are you not proud of me? I'm just practicing what you taught me."

"Casey, I taught you the healing aspects of Obeah, and I taught you that in honor of our heritage. Leave it to you to turn lightness into darkness," Amanda said, shaking her head. "If you are somewhere in a closet hiding away, using other people's bodies as puppets, is that really a life? Is this the place you've found? Are you really living your best life—breaking laws, risking going to court, losing your business, and possibly jail...worse off, hell? There is going to come a time and place where you'll have to answer to all of your wrongdoings."

Casey went silent, and William fell onto the couch into a deep sleep. He continued to sleep even after the healing work performed on him.

Sabine drove home with William around 7:30 p.m. Malik stopped by the café to help him into her car. He followed Sabine and Amanda to Sabine's house to help William to the guest room bed. William was still so out of it—it was like he was drugged. Sabine placed a bottle of water on the night stand, along with his cell phone, then said a prayer of protection for his soul. When she came out of the room, she saw Malik grab two slices of cake from the fridge.

"Sabine, can I take these?" he asked.

"Of course. Thank you for your help today. I appreciate you, brother-in-law." Sabine hugged him and he walked out of the door.

Amanda was walking around, putting crystals in the windowsills and near the front door and back patio. Hours were spent in Sabine's office today trying to make sense of this situation and trying to understand the relationship between Amanda and Casey. All that was known at that time was that Amanda, also known as Rashida, and Casey also known as Sabryna were both the biological children of the late Samby, who practiced some type of dark art.

Amanda walked up to Sabine when she was done and said, "Samby, our biological father, died before his time, according to my mother's journal."

Sabine ushered Amanda over to the kitchen table and offered her a bottle of water. "I'm listening," she said.

"Unknown illness is what was written on his death certificate," she said as she sipped her water. "But the true cause of his sickness was due to jumping bodies, as Casey did today. The more you do it, the weaker it makes you, and eventually, it leads to death."

Sabine looked at Amanda, feeling the hurt in her heart. She loved Casey. Sabine could feel it.

Amanda told the story of Nadine Johnson, her mother. Nadine was the woman who took Casey in when she was six years old after Samby passed away. Nadine was also Samby's mistress. She had Amanda seven years before Casey was born. When Samby died, Casey's mom couldn't afford to keep her, so she gave her to

Nadine. The pictures Amanda showed Sabine at the house that had Sabryna written on the back were of Casey. Sammie and Sabine both knew Casey and Amanda as young girls.

When Nadine passed away, Casey was placed in foster care. Years later when Casey was fifteen, Amanda took an interest in her. Amanda was twenty-three at the time she moved Casey in with her. That was approximately six years after Amanda lost her baby. Casey lived with Amanda for a few years until the state stepped in and legally took custody, right before her eighteenth birthday.

"I kept tabs on Casey after the state took her from me. She moved around a lot. She went off to college and met a guy, fell in love, and they moved in together. The last time we were on good terms is when I showed up for her boyfriend's funeral. He committed suicide. That day at the funeral, I hugged Casey, and I was given insight into her situation. Her defenses were down because she was so sad. She had been raped by some acquaintances of his. He had some gambling debts, and because he couldn't pay them, the men that he owed money to, hurt Casey. That's why he committed suicide."

Sabine reached out to Amanda who had tears streaming from her eyes.

"After that day, I lost her. Casey was a different person."

"So, when we met you at the club that night, did Casey recognize you?" Sabine asked.

"Yes and no," she said, wiping her tears. "Her heart has hardened, and I believe she was more focused on her agenda that night. Plus, I have a way of cloaking myself, so to speak. We'll talk later about that. I still have a lot to teach you, Sabine. It's late. I should go." She stood. "William will be fine by the morning."

After walking Amanda to her car, Sabine walked back into the house and over to the guest room to check on William. He was still sleeping. She adjusted the covers and placed her hand on his arm to check his temperature. He felt fine. She closed the guest room door, leaving it cracked just a little and hurried off to her room for a hot, healing shower and a good night's rest.

CHAPTER 32

KELVIN'S RETURN HOME

Kelvin quietly locked the front door after closing it gently behind him. He placed his keys on the hook that read "his" and dropped his duffle bag on the floor while he took off his shoes, then stopped by the kitchen to grab an ice-cold bottled water from the refrigerator. When he looked at the clock on the stove, it read 3:30 a.m. He drank the bottled water in seconds and threw the empty plastic into the trashcan. He walked into the bedroom and over to Sabine's side and kissed her forehead before heading to the bathroom to shower.

A few hours later, Sabine awakened to find her future husband's limbs wrapped around her tightly. "Kelvin," she whispered.

He turned the opposite way, no longer gripping her body, still asleep.

She turned toward him and cupped him, moving her hand up his thigh, gripping his partially erect penis, "I missed you," she whispered.

Kelvin groaned, but remained sleep.

Sabine kissed his upper back and massaged his penis with just the amount of firmness he liked.

He turned over onto his back, giving Sabine more access to his body. From the sounds of his moans, she could tell he was enjoying it. He reached over to her breasts, which were covered with his t-shirt, then asked, "Why do you have clothes on?"

Sabine's mind wondered for a few seconds, finding it odd that she wore clothes to bed also. She normally slept naked. *Oh, William's here,* she thought. She looked at the clock. It read 6:47 a.m. "I'll be right back, sweetie. Let me use the restroom," she said as she slid out of bed and pretended to walk in the direction of the bathroom, but actually walked out of the bedroom to check on William.

When she made it to the guest room door, she knocked lightly. No answer. She pushed the door open and walked into the room. William wasn't in bed. She heard the toilet flush, and he exited the bathroom.

"Sabine, did I get drunk yesterday?" he asked as he walked over to her.

"Maybe," Sabine said.

"How did I get to your house?" he asked, yawning.

"I drove you. How are you feeling?"

"Groggy, tired," he replied and sat in a chair after grabbing his cell phone off of the night stand.

"Do you have any appointments today?" Sabine asked.

"I do. I need to get in to the office by nine a.m. I have a meeting."

"Okay. I can drive you to your car. Let me jump in the shower to get ready for work."

"My car is at the café?" he asked, still trying to figure out how he missed what seemed like the whole day.

"Yes. I'll be right back," Sabine said as she slipped off to her room. She walked into her bedroom and Kelvin was still asleep. She wondered what time he got in and if he saw William. In the shower she thought, *No, he did not see William. If he had, he would have awakened me right then.* After her shower, she walked into the kitchen. William was sitting rubbing his head.

"You okay?" she asked.

"Yeah. Just a headache."

Sabine grabbed a couple of Advils from the container in the

cabinet, a bottled water from the refrigerator, and a banana off the counter for him. "Come on. Let's go."

When she was in the car she thought of how relieved she was that Kelvin didn't find William in the house. She knew Kelvin would have never let her live it down. She would've been accused of all kinds of cheating and inappropriate behavior while he was away for work, especially now that Kelvin couldn't read her like he used to.

Thank you, God, she thought. Sabine had slipped up and almost got caught with William in her home, due to being so exhausted from yesterday's events, she forgot Kelvin told her he would be home early.

"Sabine, how many mimosas did I have?" William asked after swallowing the Advil. "All I remember is eating breakfast."

"A few," she said, lying to him. Now was definitely not the time to talk about what happened yesterday.

"Oh. I thought I could hold my liquor pretty well. Must be getting old. How much champagne do you put in those things?" he asked with a smile, then turned to look at her, "You look beautiful this morning."

"Thank you. Look at you, William. The first time I invite you to stay at my house overnight, you pass out," she said, shaking her head. "Party pooper."

He laughed, then said, "Had I stayed awake, could we have continued where we left off the other night?"

"I guess you'll never know."

"Oh, I'll have another chance, I'm sure of it." He smiled.

At least William seemed to be coming out of his haze.

CHAPTER 33

REFLECTION

SABINE

Sabine walked upstairs to her office and turned the computer on. The crew was downstairs preparing for the day. She could hear Sammie walking up the stairs. She knocked on the door.

"Come in," Sabine yelled.

"Good morning," Sammie said then looked up at her sister as if something was weighing heavily on her mind.

"What's wrong?"

"Sabine, I feel so sick. I'm so nauseated," she complained then laid out across the sofa.

"That's what happens when you get knocked up," Sabine joked.

"Seriously, girl, I don't know if I can do this. I wonder how long this morning sickness lasts. It's really not morning sickness, it's all day sickness—it's on and off throughout the day."

Sabine reached into her drawer, grabbed her purse, then handed Samantha a whole bottle of antacids. Sammie chewed two immediately.

Sabine also handed her the banana sitting on the desk that was meant for William.

Sammie took a bite, then looked at Sabine, most likely wanting to decompress from yesterday.

"So, you and Malik are good now?" Sabine asked.

"Yes. I think this baby—" she touched her stomach—"is bringing us together."

"That's really good, girl."

"So, about yesterday—"

"Sammie, oh my God."

"That situation yesterday was freakier than that situation with Casey at the police station," Sammie says reflecting on when Sabine witnessed in person and Sammie witnessed over video phone, Casey's body being invaded by someone or something else, a few weeks back.

"I know, right? Did you tell Malik?"

"No. We're doing so well now. We're in such a good place. To bring up Casey now would cause all hell to break loose. Plus, I don't know if he could handle it—she scares him. That situation scares me. I'm still reeling off it myself."

"I know, right?"

"How is William?" Samantha asked. "Did he say anything about yesterday?"

"He doesn't remember. He thinks he got drunk and that's why he stayed the night at my house.

"Yeah, that's what I told Malik, that he was drunk."

"Great minds think alike," Sabine said with a half-smile.

"How are you and Kelvin?" Sammie asked.

"Good," Sabine replied, then looked down at her desk twiddling with her fingers.

"Sabine, Casey was telling it all through William yesterday, and this is the second time I've heard about you and William kissing," she said with an eyebrow raised. "Are you sure everything is good in paradise?"

Sabine shrugged.

"If you want to talk, I'm here," Sammie said then lifted herself off the sofa. "Thanks for the Tums." She shook the bottle. "I feel better now. I should go start my day," she said and exits Sabine's office.

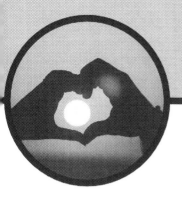

CHAPTER 34

THE REVELATION

Sabine made it home after a long day of work. She was tired and slightly irritable. The events of yesterday were starting to catch up with her. She arrived home to an empty house at 9:30 in the evening—Kelvin's jeep wasn't in the driveway. She spoke to Kelvin around noon when he woke up. He was going into the office to take care of a few things. To calm her nerves, Sabine decided to do what she did best: cook.

She put her things away and took a quick shower to wash the day off her. She grabbed the cabbage out of the refrigerator and began chopping. The phone rang. She lifted her cell phone off the counter to look at who was calling. No one. The ring was coming from the bedroom. Kelvin left his phone on the night stand. Sabine picked up the phone and looked at the caller ID. It read *Jacksonville Dispatcher*. She answered.

"Frey Transportation. May I help you?" Sabine asked.

There was silence for a few seconds, then, "Is Kelvin available?"

"He isn't available at the moment. May I take a message?"

"Can you tell him to call Darleen Smiley from Waves Logistics?"

"I will get the message to him."

"Okay," Darleen said hesitantly, then asked, "Are you like an answering service or something?"

"Ummm, no."

"Okay, because I thought this was Kelvin's cell phone. Does he have his phone forwarded someplace?"

"You are correct. This is Kelvin's cell phone. It's not forwarded. He left it at home. If you need me to get a message to him urgent, I can," Sabine said.

"Home?"

"Yes," Sabine answered irritated, becoming more frustrated at this woman's questions and suspicious as to why she was asking so many.

"Just tell him I left him a gift in his duffle bag." Darleen hung up the phone.

Sabine stood there for a while, taking in what had just happened and what she felt this woman was possibly alluding to. Sabine's feet begin to move automatically, walking over to the duffle bag near the front door, which she'd passed on her way in to the house. She grabbed it and searched through its contents—receipts, quotes, more paperwork. She unzipped the side pocket and saw a piece of neatly folded cloth. She pulled it out of the bag. Attached to it was a handwritten note that read:

> I'm glad you enjoyed the oxtails. I'm sorry I was not able to invite you over to my place, but the hotel sufficed. Here is a little token so you don't forget about me. Don't wait as long as you did before. Come see me whenever you're in Jacksonville. Like I said, you don't need to stay in a hotel. My place is always open.
>
> Darleen ☺

Sabine dropped the note and opened the cloth. What she saw, threw her off guard even more than she already was. What she thought was a cloth was actually a pair of hot pink Victoria Secret's panties.

Kelvin opened the front door a few seconds later to see Sabine standing there with a pair of pink panties in her hand. He looked down to the floor, grabbed the note, read it hurriedly, then looked back up to her with pleading eyes. "Sabine, let me explain."

THE END.

BOOK THREE IS COMING SOON.

"I am afraid of how out of control I feel in relation to
my feelings for him. He is here with me physically
tonight, but emotionally, he seems absent."
—SABINE STALLWORTH

NOTE FROM THE AUTHOR

It has been a pleasure writing this book. I am so grateful beyond what I could have ever imagined in this process of writing. It's the essence of the idea that I had as a little girl about how I would feel as an adult. What that tells me is I'm blessed to be doing what I feel is a part of my calling this lifetime. This goes hand in hand with that saying, "It doesn't feel like work when you are doing something you enjoy." That's the emotional space I'm in right now, and I'm so grateful to God for my family, friends, and to the energy of creativity and love.

If you want to keep up on the projects I'm working on, visit my website at http://shontellharris30.wixsite.com/novels. I'm currently working on the last book of *The Story of Us* series entitled, *Between Two Worlds, The Real Fairytale Ending*. I hope my books inspire, teach, and excite your senses. I'm interested in knowing what you think. Email me at S.L.Harrisnovels@gmail.com and we can talk.

Again, thank you so much for your support. It means more to me than you know. I am forever grateful.

Light and love and many blessings,

S.L. HARRIS

Printed in the United States
By Bookmasters